THE ABBEY AT VALCOURT

THE ABBEY AT VALCOURT

R. Brooke Jeffrey, MD

iUniverse, Inc.
New York Lincoln Shanghai

THE ABBEY AT VALCOURT

iUniverse books may be ordered through booksellers or by contacting:

iUniverse
2021 Pine Lake Road, Suite 100
Lincoln, NE 68512
www.iuniverse.com
1-800-Authors (1-800-288-4677)

ISBN-13: 978-0-595-37696-4 (pbk)
ISBN-13: 978-0-595-82079-5 (ebk)
ISBN-10: 0-595-37696-7 (pbk)
ISBN-10: 0-595-82079-4 (ebk)

Printed in the United States of America

Dedicated to the memory of my grandfather, Robert H. Jeffrey, MD, an American surgeon who served in the British army in WWI.

PART I

▼

CHAPTER 1

▼

Paris, May, 1917

All the glittering upper crust of Parisian society was there. The occasion was the opening night of Jean Cocteau's avant-garde ballet *Parade*. The dissonant music of Erik Satie, the staccato motion of the Negro dancers, and the cubist sets by Picasso were all intended to assault the comfortable tastes of the assembled minor nobility. In this they achieved a stunning success. The ballet was greeted first by gasps of disbelief, then muffled derision, and finally a crescendo of outrage. As the curtain descended, a full-scale riot erupted as bejeweled countesses began pummeling vainglorious artists with their oriental fans shouting, "Destroyers! Communists! Assassins!"

Amid the melee, the experimental poet Guillaume Apollinaire slowly rose from his orchestra seat. He stood unwaveringly erect as a lone sentinel of order in his sky blue officer's tunic. A black bandage wrapped around Apollinaire's head wound, which would later prove fatal, provided a faint visual echo of a different conflict: an entire world at war. Yet that world was only kilometers away, at the front in northern France. There, the assassins were not artists stridently searching for the voice of modernity; there, the destruction was all too real. The rebels Picasso and Cocteau might in time transform the old aesthetic order. But shuddering in the rain-soaked trenches on the Western Front, a half-million mutinous French soldiers might change the course of history.

CHAPTER 2

▼

By the spring of 1917, after nearly three years of unremitting slaughter on the Western Front, the French army had sustained over two million dead and wounded. The "grande armee" of poilus that had confidently marched off to meet the Germans in August of 1914 in their splendid scarlet pantaloons lost over three hundred thousand soldiers in the first two months of the war alone. The French High Command stubbornly refused to accept the bloodstained reality of mechanized warfare and that this conflict was fundamentally different from all other wars in human history. There was no military advantage in gallant cavalry charges or massed infantry attacks launched over open fields. For the first time, the strategic advantage was on the side of defenders well entrenched behind machine guns and high-explosive artillery. Yet in the minds of the French High Command to even plan for the defensive was not worthy of the legacy of Charlemagne and Napoleon. The Germans were not constrained by any such grandiose theory of warfare; if machine guns bled the tricolor white, then so be it.

The winter of 1917 was one of the coldest ever recorded in European history. Sentries on night watch froze to death on the parapets only to be transported in the morning through the trenches on litters like grotesque statues in a medieval procession. Their machine guns and truck engines froze as well. The German victories in the east allowed them to shift by train hundreds of guns to the Western Front. They soon increased their hours of shelling both day and night, and their long-range cannons could now intermittently hit Paris. The French High Command feared a massive German breakthrough and reduced or canceled leave for the troops that winter and early spring.

Despite the near total exhaustion of the French army, General Robert Nivelle pleaded that spring with the High Command to once again go on the attack. His offensive at Chemin des Dames in April of 1917 produced only a butcher's bill of a hundred thousand casualties and achieved nothing close to a breakthrough. The futility of this senseless carnage preyed on the minds of the poilus in their muddy trenches and slowly sapped the French army's famed élan.

By the end of May 1917 there were persistent rumors of yet another planned offensive. Mutiny suddenly broke out in fifty-four divisions, nearly half the French army. The men threw down their weapons, left the trenches, and refused their officer's orders. At the height of the mutiny, only two dependable divisions protected Paris from a million German troops.

Throughout the first years of the war, generals of the French High Command were comfortably billeted well behind the front in the opulent chateaux of Chantilly. When the first reports of mutiny surfaced, however, panic gripped headquarters. The mutinies coincided with a long anticipated British offensive in Flanders with over three hundred of its newest tanks and eight crack infantry divisions committed to the assault. If the Germans simultaneously attacked the depleted French lines and flanked the British, their advance would crush the one remaining Allied army with the will to fight.

At 7:30 AM on an overcast May morning, Major Henri Juffray, aide-de-camp to Supreme Commander General Foch, pushed back his chair from the massive oak table in the war room in Chateau Dauphin. He lit a cigarette to steady his nerves from a mild hangover. The converted grand ballroom with its gold leaf ceiling, pink marble columns, and murals from antiquity seemed as unreal to him as the unfolding mutiny. Despite the clamor of a dozen aides shouting over telephone lines, two lieutenants holding fistfuls of dispatches calmly proceeded to pin small red flags on the map indicating the positions of the deserting French troops.

Juffray retrieved a small fragment of tobacco from his upper lip with his left hand. In the process he glanced with disfavor at the coalescing brown spots on the aging skin of his thumb. He allowed himself one brief interlude of anguished personal vanity. He then slowly turned his torso to his right and forced himself to concentrate on the enormous battlefield map of the front. After a few minutes, Juffray suddenly rose to his feet with a purpose. His finger quickly traced an uninterrupted arc coinciding with the long line of the French trenches, which were dotted with flags as they trailed northward into British-held Flanders. Then suddenly recognizing the French regiment deployed on the extreme right British flank, he gasped and spoke unconsciously out loud, "My God!" Startled, he turned and shouted to the adjoining officer manning the phones, "Hevert, Hevert, listen to me. The Moroccans, the Second Army at Valcourt. When did we last reinforce them?"

Major Jean Hevert did not look up from his neatly stacked pile of dispatches. His cynical reply came in an emotionless monotone, pressing forward a small cloud of cigarette smoke, "My good fellow, when did we ever reinforce them?"

CHAPTER 3

▼

His mind made a slow, effortless transition from the comforting amnesia of sleep to a gradual awareness of his surroundings. The morning chill on his exposed forehead, the gray-green shaft of light by the steps of the dugout, the moisture dripping below his nostrils, and the pressure on his bladder were all preempted by the ascending seizure in his lungs. Lieutenant Allain Rennaut of the 3d Moroccan battalion, known simply as the Troisième, struggled to his feet and coughed violently as he flung open the makeshift curtain by his canvass cot, located fifteen feet below ground. Shivering in his nightshirt, he instinctively covered his mouth as he coughed again and again. His face turned red with this sudden and uncontrollable hacking, which left him hungering for air. It was his morning paroxysm of trench cough; a cough that could rip the fibers of your chest muscles until you slumped to your knees like a penitent thief begging for communion. It was the price one paid for a life underground in perpetual dampness to escape the nightly shelling.

When Rennaut recovered sufficiently and could breathe calmly again, he repeatedly rubbed his nightshirt to wipe off the dripping moisture from the earthen walls. He lit a small kerosene lamp and then poured some sour milk into a fragmented shell casing for the stray calico kitten that slept in his padded steel helmet.

"The earth is weeping for us both, little one," Rennaut said as he stroked its roughed clumps of matted orange fur. A cat might be a good thing to have it reflected, but then with the rats in the trenches nearly twice its size, where was the advantage? He wondered, as he lightly stroked the underside of its chin, if the kitten's fate subtly mirrored his own.

He then stared intently around the disheveled dugout and tried to recalibrate his senses. His sense of smell had long since vanished in the dank underground. The coffee and cognac in a tin cup on the crate that served as a makeshift table, the half-empty can of tobacco, the brown-stained cloth used to clean his revolver, and his shirt—stiffened from the frozen sweat of his armpits—were all sterile two-dimensional objects to him without their pungent smells. He had grown impervious to the power of the ubiquitous mold and was only briefly aware of its sickening stench when he first reentered the dugout each night after dark to sleep.

On the table was Rennaut's unfinished correspondence. There were letters to the relatives of the men in his company killed in the shelling over the past three days. The letters were addressed to Bedouin villages in the Atlas Mountains or alleyways in Tangiers, where few spoke French and fewer still had heard of the Western Front. The Muslim shopkeepers in the bazaars talked over their thick black coffee with their prayer beads in their hands. They understood the irony that their sons had volunteered for a great crusade to help their Christian masters. But why? The world must be truly mad they thought and they consciously hid such reflections from their wives who still held out hope that their sons might soon return.

In middle age, Rennaut's fingers did not respond easily in the morning chill. The buttons on his tunic bedeviled him as he dressed unconsciously. He headed first for the latrine and then the field mess to retrieve his cup of coffee and several baguettes for the men on sentry duty.

Rennaut had slept fitfully as rumors spread through the battalion that some men of the 67th infantry, dug in on their right flank, and the artillery battalion, in reserve, were refusing orders and leaving the trenches. Over the past three days, a pamphlet containing communist slogans urging mutiny had secretly circulated among the men. The night before, Rennaut had heard a sergeant from the 119th artillery battalion address the Arab troops. A thin and willowy man with a resonant voice, Sergeant Mouton stood on the running board of a Model T ambulance in a frayed, mud-caked tunic and delivered a speech to a crowd of fifty soldiers. As soon as he began, some of the junior officers reported him to the ranking frontline officer of the 3d Moroccan, Captain Michel Hassan, and asked permission to arrest him on the spot.

Hassan had refused by saying, "Let him speak his mind. Treason is an action. It is not a string of words. It is better that the men hear of the mutiny and decide for themselves."

Mouton had closed his speech by shouting, "For three long years now the generals sleeping on their silk sheets have repeatedly ordered us to charge the machine guns. And for what? For this pile of mud? For these millions dead? We will defend France, but comrades join us! Join us in saying no! No to charging the machine guns!"

Rennaut was bewildered by it all. A mutiny by his men in the Troisième seemed unthinkable to him, but still he wondered—if it could happen in the 67th and 119th, there was a lingering uncertainty. He also knew by the volume of ammunition and matériel coming through the railway depot in Valcourt that something big was going to happen in the British sector. They held the English flank and the entire operation would be at risk if the Germans broke through at Valcourt.

Rennaut began to make his rounds distributing baguettes through the communications trenches, calmly hailing the lethargic sentries like patrons of a working class bistro after a heavy night. He wondered aloud to himself about the fate of Sergeant Mahmoud and his night patrol to capture German sentries. There had been no concerted attacks in the past two weeks. Both he and Captain Hassan feared that during this lull reinforcements might be diverted from the German victories on the eastern front and fuel a new assault. With the spring rains and constant cloud cover, aerial reconnaissance was limited at best. Only new German prisoners could provide the clues to the timing of the next attack.

A stocky, robust man of forty-four, Rennaut's gray eyes and bushy moustache seemed to fade into the blue of his greatcoat after so many years in the army. When a new Moroccan battalion was first assembled in Marseilles in early 1915, the High Command knew that experienced French officers held the key to their survival at the front and Rennaut was transferred from Toulon to assist in the difficult training of the men.

The army was Rennaut's entire adult frame of reference. Over the course of two decades, he had been promoted to captain twice, but each time was subsequently demoted for disobedience, drunkenness, or general unsuitability for senior command. His brief civilian life held different disappointments, and he had in succession failed as a print setter, cloth importer, and gunrunner in the Sudan. Long forgotten was a failed marriage with only a rare letter requesting money as a distant reminder that there had been a time when he had not worn scarlet pants.

He had not taken part in the prior evening's discussions, but Rennaut had overheard the men at their campfires after Mouton's speech talking quietly, sometimes in broken French, sometimes in Arabic. What he could understand of their conversation rang true to him as an old soldier. The men did not hold a grudge against the Germans or understand why or how the war had started. Few of them in their remote villages had even known there was a Germany before the outbreak of war. They only knew that, like the French and British, the Germans were white Europeans and, therefore, desired to rule the dark peoples. But the men and boys of the Troisième had chosen to join the army and escape a crushing life devoid of opportunity or adventure. Morale was unusually high in the battalion as the men felt bound not by a social class or by an ideology, but by their shared experiences as outsiders and, most importantly, by their faith in the decency of their officers. They had come to France to fight, perhaps to die. If other men wanted to desert, that was their business and they would bear the consequences. No one in the Troisième believed in the glory of France or believed in the wisdom of charging machine guns. But they believed in Captain Hassan and not in communist slogans.

Rennaut had never believed in the glory of anything. Within his self-contained universe of the army, surrounded by death for so long, he had come to see things purely based on a cruel immediacy. Reflection on larger issues would be left to those not at the front, for whom life held future possibilities beyond the capricious landing of the next artillery shell. Three years of war had obliterated the past as well as any thoughts of the future. His focus and passion was improving the men's life in the trenches today; they might all be dead tomorrow. This gradually became his total preoccupation and he knew in his deepest thoughts that his devotion to this task had enabled him to somehow preserve his sanity during the perpetual madness of the war.

Rennaut instinctively understood what mattered most to the men. All soldiers had common needs and desires, whether they came from small Arab villages or the slums of Marseilles. He would be quick to acknowledge that some important things were beyond his control. First and most important to the men was the confidence in their leaders. As a lieutenant, he could only partly provide this to his own company, but as long as Captain Hassan was alive, the entire battalion would be in good hands. Their previous well-liked commanding officer, Captain Charles Robine, had survived the carnage of Verdun and the Somme in 1916 only to be gassed to death three months ago when a stray chlorine shell landed just outside his dugout, during the early fighting for Valcourt. Robine had recognized Corporal Hassan's leadership skills under fire and had him rapidly promoted to second and then first lieutenant over modest objections from the High Command. There were some who felt that the Arab half-breed's rise was too accelerated. Yet when Robine was killed and there were no other officers with the right credentials to spare, they had no alternative but to promote him to captain. Major Albert Gastineau and Colonel Georges Lefevre, the nominal battalion commanders of the Troisième, were billeted miles away from the front and rarely visited the troops. They left day-to-day command to Captain Hassan, who led by example and always urged Rennaut to think creatively about the welfare of the men. When necessary, he looked the other way when some of Rennaut's methods were not precisely sanctioned by army regulations.

Despite months of constant German shelling, one wall of the Montebrillion abbey on the outskirts of Valcourt remained standing. The eastern wall still supported its small, but masterful stained glass windows. At the apex of the window in a brilliant arc of mosaics was a depiction of the Christian triumvirate of the Father, Son, and Holy Ghost. But in the subterranean mire of the trenches, Rennaut held fast to his own Holy Trinity on the Western Front: dry boots, hot stew, and a clean, well-sighted rifle.

With the spring thaw and accompanying rains, Rennaut's highest priority was the men's feet and keeping the trenches dry. Wet trenches dramatically increased the rat population and with them came lice, typhus, and fever. Rennaut knew that an even greater threat to morale was trench foot. He had seen firsthand that men temporarily overcome by fear or shell shock could be regrouped and with strong leadership be reorganized into an effective fighting force. Rennaut understood, however, that no matter how brave, a man preyed upon by the constant, diabolic pain of swollen and necrotic toes was no longer any use as a soldier.

Rennaut was continuously directing measures to build retaining walls along the ridge beneath the abbey and to line the bottom of the main trenches. This required straw, gravel, and most importantly wooden planks to be made into duckboards. The wood was "commandeered" from local farmers who were bribed with war booty to let his men tear down any barn or out building not of the highest priority. His supreme logistical challenge, however, was the row of trenches along their northern flank, parallel to the Ancre River, a veritable swamp of marshes, willows, and endless natural springs. Digging a trench to the required depth of eight feet to withstand shelling and sniper fire inevitably resulted in a foot or more of muddy water at its bottom. The solution to this problem required all the technical, political, and financial skills of a lifelong army outlaw willing to risk court-martial or a firing squad to pull off the bribes and thievery required. Rubber tubing was "liberated" from American Field Service ambulance tires, pumps and compressors obtained through barter from British engineers, and gas-fired electric generators procured from black market

French war profiteers. All of these components were all painstakingly acquired through complex parallel operations. Marveling at the sight of the swampy trench pumped dry for the first time, Rennaut somehow wondered to himself that if only he had been in charge of the international negotiations after the assassination in the Balkans, then perhaps he would still be back in the Sudan trafficking used Mauser rifles.

It nevertheless took four hours of constant pumping to bring down the water to manageable levels in the trenches. Because of the loud noise, Captain Hassan ordered Rennaut to operate the pumps only during the hours of fairly predictable German shelling—from around 8:30 AM to noon. This would ensure that no staff officers from the chateau would be at the front lines inspecting the troops and discover Rennaut's contraband. On one occasion when Major Gastineau marveled to Rennaut about the quality of the river trench line, Rennaut exclaimed with great deference, "It's our French soil, sir. It produces the finest straw in the world!"

Despite all his devotion to the trenches, Rennaut realized that an equally high priority after three years of war was fresh meat for stew. Rennaut knew that men with dry boots and hot stew could fight on indefinitely under reasonable officers. By 1917 the once plentiful herds of livestock on farms near the front had long been depleted. The brutally cold winter had been devastating and the few chickens and cows secretly hidden by the farmers for their own families had all but disappeared.

The standard French army issue of 350 grams per day of highly salted canned beef "singe" (monkey meat) was largely inedible to the North Africans. For the French troops the "singe" could only be made palatable by washing it down with large quantities of rough red wine known as "pinard," or bull's piss. This alcoholic option, however, was not a possibility for the Muslim men of the Troisième.

Fresh stew meat was relatively plentiful in wartime Paris. Getting it to the front, however, was an immense challenge because the French government was under severe criticism from the public for tolerating even modest levels of black market war profiteering. It took all of Rennaut's creative genius to master the supply problem of fresh meat that drew upon his considerable resources from civilian and army life. Once a week, forged vouchers were produced by his old printing contacts in Paris. Through a series of elaborate intermediaries, these vouchers gained access to butchers on the fringes of Les Halles. Truck drivers were then bribed with a precious black market metal: German tin alloy shell casings to be pounded into the latest craze of the Parisian bourgeoisie, cigarette lighters. This graft lubricated the wheels of French army camions transporting meat from Paris to a secret rendezvous five miles south of the field hospital near Chevregny. At that point, American Red Cross ambulances, with their adventurous Ivy League drivers, were easy to enlist in the crusade. They were routinely waived through the checkpoints at the front by the military police for the transport of "humanitarian" supplies.

Rennaut also firmly believed in a clean, well-sighted Lee Enfield rifle. Standard issue to the British infantry, the Lee Enfield held a ten-round clip that could easily be reloaded under fire. The Lee Enfield was far superior in accuracy and firepower to the latest issue French rifle, the Berthier, which could hold only six bullets in its magazine. A well-trained infantry marksman with the Lee Enfield could accurately aim and shoot fifteen rounds a minute. By comparison, the standard issue 8-mm St. Etienne machine guns fired clips of twenty-four rounds a minute and required a skilled assistant to rapidly reload. In fact, in earlier battles, charging German infantry mistook the withering number of bullets from the Lee Enfield for machine gun fire and abandoned their attack. The Moroccan battalion was chronically short of machine guns and Rennaut knew that the Lee Enfield rifle had been one of the keys to their success in repelling three German attacks in the past two months. Bartering for the Lee Enfield and its ammunition from cockney British master sergeants was surprisingly easy. The going rate was ten Lee Enfields for a single case of champagne.

Shortly after 7:00 AM, Rennaut finished his walk through the frontline trench inquiring of the men in muffled, cheerful tones and bringing loaves of crusted bread to the corporals in charge. As he slowly ascended the switchbacks of crude earthen steps along the ridgeline to the lookout post, he paused midway and gazed skyward at the cloud cover and mist. "No reconnaissance planes again today," he said to himself.

He stopped for a moment when he thought he noticed something and looked skyward again. He began to observe a large gray hawk circling effortlessly in a slowly widening, graceful circle over the ruined abbey. The motionless wings of the gliding bird seemed somehow irrational to Rennaut, defying both gravity and natural law.

"Hunting early, or just putting your prey on notice?" he wondered.

As he watched the bird for a few moments, he noticed that its arc spanned the verdant springtime foliage east of the abbey to the muddy barrenness of no man's land. Tracing the bird's flight, he began to notice an extreme contrast in color. On the battlefield there was a complete absence of the color green. Only a few blackened and denuded trunks stood out from the sea of brown mud. They jutted out between mounds of barbed wire looking more like grave markers than trees. He noticed that the hawk suddenly came to rest on a charred branch of one of the few remaining trees taller than the height of a man. Two branches twisted outward from its trunk like a macabre crucifix. He raised his field glasses to get a closer look at the hawk when, in an instant, a shot from a German sentry's rifle shattered the branch, and the bird quickly fled aloft.

Rennaut then continued his climb and as he reached the lookout post beneath the abbey walls he glanced at his pocket watch. It was nearly 7:20 AM. He grew apprehensive about entering his most difficult time of the day, the time between his morning rounds and the predictable German shelling after stand-in at 8:15 AM. The bursting shells were a daily reminder that this was not a dream, but a continuation of the meaningless conflict. During the first two years of the war, he dreaded this brief moment of time more than any other. He was not alone in that fear and had once overheard Captain Robine refer to it as the "soldier's purgatory." The soldier awoke each morning, with an irrational, but instinctive feeling of hope. There were, of course, constant symbols of the military and reminders of the war everywhere—the uniforms, the salutes, the weapons, the incessant orders. But sleep induces a subtle forgetfulness; for the briefest moment it diminishes the immediacy of the war. The reality of the war cruelly returns after the crashing of the first shell. No, the war seemed intractable and inevitable as long as a few men dug in deep in the earth survived and were determined to continue it.

Rennaut for several years dealt with this "purgatory" by pouring a liberal dose of cognac into his morning coffee. "Good for the cough," he'd say to the onlooking Arab boys. But over time, more and more alcohol was required to quell his anxiety surrounding the resumption of the shelling. The Germans in late February launched a surprise morning attack despite intelligence reports assuring High Command that they were retreating. After the opening barrage, Captain Robine found him drunk at his sentry post. Rennaut rallied through his alcoholic haze and acted on instinct and nerve to organize the defenses as best he could, but he knew he had let the battalion down. The French line wavered, but ultimately held. Hassan, however, was badly wounded in the shoulder and neck and Captain Robine was killed. As illogical as it might seem, Rennaut blamed himself for the casualties.

Scanning the desolate earth from the lookout point, Rennaut's mind kept coming back to that humiliating time of his drunkenness. He thought, "Why must I constantly dwell on this unpleasantness? Why won't it go away?" Yet another scene from that time haunted him as well. After Hassan had been wounded and transported to the field hospital, the task had fallen to Rennaut to collect Captain Robine's personal effects from his dugout and forward them to his widow. Robine had been regular army his entire adult life and was held in high esteem by the men for his professionalism and concern for their well-being. Rennaut had met few other commanders during his long tenure in the army who had earned such respect. Quieter than most, with a mild speech impediment, Robine had none of the feigned bravado of the High Command. He would never press an obviously futile attack despite direct orders to the contrary. His style of leadership among his officers was first to review the intelligence estimates and then to ask each company commander for an overall assessment. After hearing all the arguments, he would simply lay out a coordinated military plan by stating, "I think this is best." When the German infantry had nearly broken through the 67th battalion four months ago, it was Robine who recognized the danger, personally took charge, and repositioned the artillery and machine guns at the critical moment to turn the tide.

With Hassan gravely injured, it fell to Rennaut to inventory Robine's personal belongings. He remembered lighting a kerosene lamp and surveying Robine's dugout and thinking to himself just how ordinary it was and how little his surroundings reflected the greatness of the man. He was startled to find that it looked no different that the other bunkers at the front with its cloth cot, regulation wool blankets, two small armoires, and wooden table and chair. Rennaut knew that Robine had turned down a position as adjuvant to Colonel Lefevre at his chateau rather than be separated from the men. The extent of his sacrifice was now clearly evident to Rennaut. He was surprised at just how few things were left to account for Robine's long years in the service. One armoire with several hangers held a few odd pieces of clothing, an extra uniform, and pair of boots. On the table were a few family pictures, a pen, and several unfinished letters home to the battalion's newest widows. The other armoire, however, contained a rather startling surprise; it had been converted into a bookcase, and every square inch of its four shelves was full of novels and books of poetry. He quickly scanned the top three shelves, which displayed volumes by Tolstoy, Flaubert, Dostoyevsky, and Hugo as well as numerous books of poetry by Baudelaire, Whitman, and the English romantics. The bottom shelf, however, contained only one small leather-bound book. It appeared very worn, but had no title. Rennaut took it down with some apprehension and began to read. It was Robine's diary. Each entry was recorded by the day and time. Many of the pages concerned routine military matters. However, Rennaut noticed a daily pattern and that the entry at 7:30 AM invariably had lines of verse with no titles. Robine had spent his time in "purgatory" writing poetry. He knew Captain Hassan used this time for sketching and painting; how would he fill his own time? Rennaut read Robine's last diary entry:

February 6, 1917, 7:30 AM.

> I measure time quite differently now,
> Not in weeks or hours,
> Or falling grains of sand
> But the number
> Of memories of you,
> I still can recall.
> Memories,
> Like signposts
> On a distant road,
> We once shared.
> Will we ever travel
> That road again?

CHAPTER 4

▼

As the darkness in the early morning sky gave way to an ambiguous gray, Private Achmed Mansour reached underneath his cot and retrieved a brightly painted blue matchbox. He carefully selected a single match and shivered in the morning air as he lit the nub of the candle on his nightstand. Mansour then peered into the shadows at the end of the bed until he saw the profile of the dog that he had recently adopted. The beagle raised his left ear reluctantly without moving his face nestled in his paws. The gesture was intended to feign acknowledgement of a new day, but was sufficiently restrained to indicate that a few more hours of rest were in order. Mansour smiled at the dozing animal through the ribbons of grayish light, stroked its neck, and then peered once again into the matchbox. He carefully extracted a precious object and held it firmly in his clasped hands and as he approached the diminutive iron stove at the end of the dugout. He prayed to Allah and then to the fire gods to make possible the heat for Captain Hassan's tea.

Mansour was judged by the French army recruiters to be "too simple" for regular infantry duty, and over the past decade of service—first in the Foreign Legion and later the army—he worked as a cook, a stable hand, and a soup bearer. Mansour's exact age was difficult to ascertain, but the thick silver strands marbling his unkempt beard suggested that he, like the other few who survived at the front, had aged rapidly in its subterranean environment. Nearly as tall, but much heavier than Hassan, Mansour's shoulders were rounded and stooped as if weathered by some force of nature. Yet he was known throughout the battalion for his prodigious physical strength. Once when an artillery formation supporting the Troisième took a direct hit, several guns were thrown up in the air, crushing the leg of a young soldier. Mansour single-handedly lifted up the wheel axles so Corporal Sayed could extract the wounded gunner.

Mansour's childlike indifference to the war and joy in performing small daily tasks was an annoyance to some and a mystery to others. It set him apart from the men in the trenches, who were living in constant fear and deprivation. Everyone in the battalion it seems knew about his frequent and seemingly inappropriate smiling. It would begin with a slow vertical parting of the lips and the high-pitched utterance "ohhhh" and then proceed with an enormous horizontal finish exposing his sparse lower teeth and the low-pitched sound "ahhh." That Mansour could smile equally at both insignificant and frightful events became accepted by the men and often diffused moments of extreme fear and tension.

Sergeant Mahmoud was the first to recognize Mansour's special status. At a gathering of the Troisième's Arab elders at a late-night campfire, he identified his unique quality: "Mansour cannot comprehend the horror of the war. He does not wish death, but unlike any of us, he does not fear it."

The elders subtly began to take notice of Mansour and in the process observed an even more important quality. Mansour's "simplicity" seemed forged from a fundamental goodness, devoid of the cynical complexities derived from higher levels of thought: guile, deception, ennui, and paralyzing self-doubt. Mansour, moreover, seemed to the elders to be touched by the "hand of Allah." On several occasions during artillery barrages Mansour was noted to be somehow impervious to harm. Once during a particularly intense bombardment, Mansour was huddled shoulder to shoulder with fifteen other men in a deep underground bunker. The shelling went on for hours; men quietly sobbed, pounded the earthen walls in anger, gasped for air in claustrophobic terror, or soiled themselves in their helplessness. Mansour suddenly stood up and asked earnestly for silence. He listened for a moment and then left the bunker and returned twenty minutes later with the head of a small beagle pup protruding from his partially buttoned tunic. Corporal Mustaf observed the entire episode through field glasses from his lookout post below the abbey. He told the rest of the company over the campfire that night that shells burst on nearly every inch of ground except the path walked by Mansour.

It was decided by the Arab elders of the Troisième that Mansour would be designated as Captain Hassan's "personal attaché." English officers were individually assigned batmen who functioned as private valets at the front. The French, true to their spirit of "egalité" eschewed such aristocratic vestiges at lower officer levels. Hassan had been wounded twice in the last four months and every man in the Troisième greatly feared for his life. Something out of the ordinary needed to be done to shield him. Captain Robine had been a fine officer living with the men and sharing their deprivations. His death left a cloud of depression over the battalion until Hassan was put in command. As a sergeant, Hassan had volunteered for the Troisième when it was first commissioned and in three years had become nearly fluent in Arabic. His linguistic skills allowed him to reach out to the men in quiet conversations. It was not just that Hassan was a brother, being part Arab. After all, he did not follow the Koran and was often seen painting the Christian abbey and even drinking alcohol. No, it was something else the elders could not precisely define. Perhaps they sensed in him something that gave them hope for the future and that he somehow would get them through this nightmare of a war. Hope was in short supply that winter in the frozen trenches with the constant shelling, frostbite, and the closeness of death. Perhaps too they saw in Hassan a connection between the modern world and what little was worth preserving from the past.

The men of the Troisième were well aware of the alarming casualty rate among their officers. Indeed, the lieutenants and captains who lead the infantry charges over the top into battle armed with only a whistle and a revolver suffered staggering losses in every attack. Given the danger, something had to be done to protect Hassan. His pointless killing in the wake of Robine's death would bring about an almost unbearable suffering in this, the cruelest of wars. Without Hassan, the unthinkable, the abyss, even mutiny, might be a possibility in the Troisième. The elders—Sayed, Mahmoud, and Mustaf—saw in Private Mansour the shield of Allah's hand. It was decided that Mansour would sleep on a cot near the small kitchen in Hassan's dugout and would shadow the captain in combat. It was hoped that his presence and aura as a "blessed one" would somehow create a barrier of protection around Hassan.

As the water slowly began to boil, Captain Hassan buttoned his shirt and sat down at the small wooden table next to Mansour. Mansour selected a tea bag that had been used only three times before and placed it lovingly into the tin mess cup, "Will you be riding today, Captain?" Mansour asked.

"Yes, Leconde and I will ride over to the 67th. There are difficulties there and sooner or later the Germans will…well, we can't expect this lull to last much longer."

"Yes, the 67th needs help. You can always tell by the way that man walks," replied Mansour as he began to grin.

"What do you mean, Mansour?" asked Hassan sipping the hot tea-flavored water.

"Scared officers always walk that way, Captain. You know, with their chest stuck out I mean. Isn't that right, Bijoux? Don't they walk like that, little one?" he said stroking the dog's head as it rubbed against Mansour's leg.

Mansour turned and smiled again and as he sliced a piece of bread. "They want the abbey, sir. The Germans, I mean."

"The abbey, Mansour? Perhaps, but I suspect they want the railroad junction just as much."

"Oh no, Captain. There, you are wrong. They can always make another railroad. The Boche are good at that, but not the windows. They can't make the windows. Bijoux and I know that. I will have the horse ready after your sketching, Captain."

As Mansour left to ready his horse, Captain Hassan gulped his tea and headed for the latrine. He then went to the dugout in the communications trench and sat for a moment to read the overnight dispatches from High Command warning of growing mutinies in the eastern sector near Verdun. After countersigning the perfunctory orders sent from Colonel Lefevre's command giving him the authority to shoot any mutineers, he folded the scrap of paper and placed it discreetly out of sight from the telegraph clerk.

Hassan gathered his charcoals and sketchpad in a leather satchel and walked into the light morning mist along a dirt path a quarter mile to the ruined abbey. For the next few minutes on his journey, Hassan consciously stopped thinking about his battalion duties and concentrated on the natural setting: a small gray squirrel darting across the path, the smell of the wet tall grass, the softness of the light filtering through the beech tress, and the feel of his boots on the damp earth.

During the first few weeks when the 3d Moroccans were dug in along the ridge in front of the abbey, they were under constant bombardment. What remained of the medieval structure after months of shelling was only a jagged section of the east wall with its relatively small but exquisitely multicolored triptych of stained glass windows. Even in modernity, the intensely brilliant hues of lapis from Afghanistan, garnet from Sicily, and amber from Niger made a startling impression; more aesthetic than devotional to some, but a profound work of craftsmanship to all. Against the fieldstone rubble of the collapsed abbey walls and the adobe-colored clay from the trench works, the windows' striking colors created a disturbing contrast, a reminder of things before this cycle of destruction. To the local farmers, the preservation of the windows seemed miraculous and linked them to a different, tranquil time.

Hassan at first saw nothing miraculous about the windows. True, he marveled at the good fortune of their safekeeping, but he had seen the death of too many fine men under random conditions to believe that their continued existence was due to anything other than chance. Over time, however, something drew him to the windows. He remembered the first time in early March when he began to visit them daily before morning stand-in. The two-dimensional figure of Christ with his outstretched arms had awakened in him a dormant memory of the medieval art in books he had admired at the small chapel of his orphanage near Chartres.

At thirty, nearly half of Hassan's life had been spent in the army and the other half in the orphanage. One intervening year had been spent painting as an apprentice in a studio in Paris. Carvalho, his art teacher, had observed as he left for the army at sixteen that he was wasting his talent and trading one faceless institution for another. But Hassan knew that a life as an artist was open to only a privileged few. Yet as an orphan, he felt comfortable in the anonymity of the army. What could he do as an Arab half-breed? What worlds were open to him? The army had been the career of the one man in the orphanage he was close to, Tommasso, the gardener. He had seen how Tommasso had cherished his army comrades and had formed close relationships that Hassan envied. Camille, the one girl he had loved at the orphanage seemed to choose a career in music over him. No, he did not regret the army as a choice. He had advanced on his merits to the level of captain, and his longing for closeness was partially fulfilled by the Arab men of the Troisième and his sketching partially fulfilled his passion for art.

The medieval windows had played a pivotal role in rekindling this passion. What especially intrigued him over time was the awareness that his emotional reaction to the windows subtly changed in different lighting. The intensity of the colors seemed to modulate in different weather and with different cloud cover in the morning. That something as permanent as the Christ, the God-figure, could evoke different responses in him with different lighting struck Hassan as a paradox at first, but he soon began to see it as the sign of a masterpiece. The windows had revived his interest in capturing these different reactions. Sketching had become the one humanistic distraction he allowed himself at the front.

Colonel Georges Lefevre, the regiment's commanding officer, was a man devoted to his distractions. An amicable, if somewhat indifferent warrior in his late sixties, the colonel was decidedly more enthusiastic about dahlias, Italian cars, and the latest vintage of Beaujolais than about complex military strategy. Lefevre had been injured in a riding accident as a cavalry officer in the Franco-Prussian War, his only semblance of combat. He rose through the ranks during peacetime more on the social connections of his wife in the drawing rooms of Paris than on his talents in the field. Comfortably pensioned at the start of the war, Lefevre was called out of retirement in 1916 as the "grand armee" grew to ninety divisions. Lefevre was assigned to command various reserve units guarding ammunition dumps or railway junctions. Insidiously, as more combat divisions were slowly drawn away to the east and south to be used in the great battles for Verdun, Lefevre found his regiment holding the end of the French line on the extreme right flank of the British.

The colonel's usual routine was to rise from his grand bedroom in the Château D'Amercy at around 10:00 AM. He would then sign a few prepared dispatches in bed, lunch from 1:00 to 3:00 PM with a few majors and desk officers and perhaps take a ride in his staff car to take in the afternoon parade if the shelling had stopped. A stroll in the late afternoon through the gardens and then an early dinner and bedtime rounded out his day. His great triumph of the past month was to convince his wife to send him the heavy tapestry curtains from their apartment in Paris to cover the twenty-foot windows in his grand bedroom at the château. Unless he could somehow muffle the sound of the devilish German shelling and get his proper rest, Lefevre feared he would have to move his headquarters further west and give up his palatial surroundings and elegant gardens.

A few minutes past 7:00 AM, his servant rushed into the bedroom blurting in barely understandable phrases, "Excuse me, Colonel, I'm so sorry, but you see, there is a telegram, sir, something about a mutiny."

Lefevre had been aware from High Command of rumors about growing restlessness among the troops. He had been in the army long enough, however, to know that a few communists or malcontents would not prevail against the might of ninety divisions, particularly if they threw down their weapons. A few well-staged executions and this entire distressing business would be over. Struggling to swing his feet across the enormous bed, Lefevre spoke in a surprisingly calm and soft voice, "What, what is this about a mutiny? This is nonsense. Get me the battalion commanders at once!"

The regiment under Lefevre's command was part of the French Second Army and included two infantry battalions (the 67th and the 3d Moroccan) and one artillery battalion (the 119th). After capturing the village of Valcourt in February, the 3d Moroccans had been dug in for twelve weeks along a ridge beneath the crumbling abbey of Montebrillion. Their trench lines paralleled the ancient Roman road leading north of the village along the river. The Moroccans had successfully repelled two German attacks in the last eight weeks, each time, however, sustaining considerable losses. Rather than the customary battalion strength of six hundred men, difficulties in reinforcements had left their ranks with barely three hundred and fifty. Lefevre was appointed regimental commander in mid-March after General Joffre had determined that the Second Army could only serve in a purely defensive role.

The hamlet of Valcourt on the Ancre River was in peacetime nothing more than a Saturday morning market for the surrounding farmers. In wartime, however, it became a vital railway and trucking hub connecting supply lines that reinforced the British to the northwest and the French to the southeast.

"What are the latest reports?" the colonel called out in a forceful, but disarmingly cheerful way. He struggled to button his officer's tunic as he strode into the converted grand dining room that served as a command center. The snarled mass of telephone lines on the great oak tables always slightly amazed Lefevre. "Oh, for the more simple time of couriers on horseback," he sighed.

A partially hidden corporal responded from within the warren of cables, "Nothing definite as yet from the Troisième or the artillery Colonel, but Captain de Clairant reports that most of the 67th have left their posts and are milling about the railroad station refusing to go back to the trenches."

"But what of Hassan and the Troisième? We must determine their status immediately!"

At the outset of the war, both France and Great Britain knew that troops from their colonies were essential to match the enormous collective might mobilized by Germany and the Austro-Hungarian Empire. French recruitment officers brandishing the promise of regular soldier's wages had relatively little difficulty raising troops from the bazaars in Tangiers or the mud-brick Bedouin villages in the Atlas Mountains. The "territorials," as they were known, at first wore their beige fezzes with red tassels until outfitted with the protective steel helmets of the "the hairy ones," the bearded poilus. The 3d Moroccan battalion fought admirably under their French officers and distinguished themselves at the Somme in 1916. As losses mounted, however, only a small number of other North African colonials as well as French Algerians reinforced the Moroccans troops. They were for the most part Arab immigrant dockworkers from Marseilles or street cleaners from Paris. Although inexperienced and barely able to grow a mustache, they were nonetheless fiercely proud to be part of the Troisième.

CHAPTER 5

▼

After breaking his baguette and telling the two sentries to go get coffee, Rennaut lifted his field glasses and scanned the German front trenches 2,000 yards across the gray-brown denuded earth. Other than the chalky spiral plumes wafting in the mist from the German campfires, there was little sign of activity. There were no obvious corpses beyond the barbed wire and this likely meant that corporal Mahmoud and his patrol had probably gotten through.

"The Boche will still be having their black bread and coffee for another half-hour, so I'll have my baguette," he thought. Dipping the firm crust into the weak coffee, he allowed his mind to wander uncontrollably. Random thoughts surfaced of his boyhood in Lyon. A street rat that knew every alleyway and escape route from the priests and truant officers—his mind raced over a collage of images and sensations. He recalled the smell of his father's bakery early in the morning, the low shadow of the rusted metal grate over the sewer where he would hide, the soft touch of a girl's taffeta confirmation dress as it lightly grazed his hand, and finally thoughts of his only boyhood friend, Maurice. The two of them were always there in the same café after school in a time removed from the anxiety of a world at war. They loved to share their excitement about their latest cycling heroes. But he then remembered Maurice had been killed at Verdun.

As he put his field glasses away, he was conscious of a slight tremor in his left hand. Rennaut spoke to himself in an abstract way, "You'll be all right now, no trouble today. Not today."

He then felt a slight sensation on his right hand as he rested his field glasses on the top of the sandbag parapet. Rennaut stopped to observe two ants crawling across his left thumb trying to transport a tiny bit of crust that had fallen from his bread. The crumb by Rennaut's rough calculation was easily twice their size. At first he thought the two ants were trying to pull the crumb along together, but on closer inspection he clearly realized that both were fiercely tugging against each other to control it. The force of one, however, neutralized the movement of the other. Finally, in a desperate move, one ant rolled on its back to try to dislodge the crumb from the other. But this upset the delicate balance between the two, and both ants tumbled back into the darkness of the trench.

At that instant, Rennaut suddenly recoiled below the trench line from the high-pitched whine of a German 88 shell. He gathered his wits while crouching in the trench and concentrated on the fire. He quickly realized by the distribution of the falling shells that it was not a rolling barrage signaling an assault, but rather just harassing target practice along the north river road leading out of town. Shelling the river road ensured that British supply convoy trucks leaving from town that morning would once again have to detour and take the much longer western road to reach Arras.

"A bit early for this nonsense," Rennaut mused to himself as he made his way again up to the parapet and fixed his field glasses on the mounds of earth spewed up along the poplar-lined road. He wondered how much repair work would be needed that afternoon to make the road passable for the evening convoy. To his astonishment he recognized a single horse-drawn carriage moving slowly up the road in mottled sunlight, thus defying the entire German artillery. He knew instantly it was Father Dierot, the local parish priest. Like Lefevre, Dierot had been recalled out of a comfortable retirement after his predecessor, Father Maigret, had been killed along with nineteen villagers who were trying to repair the abbey when its roof collapsed a year ago.

Rennaut saw the exploding shells bracketing the carriage a hundred feet in front and then a hundred feet behind. Dierot and his horse kept up a slow but determined pace until the carriage reached the forward French lines. Rennaut left the observation post and ran to the first trenches. As a corporal grabbed the reins of Father Dierot's horse, Rennaut rushed to speak to him, "Father, haven't I told you a thousand times to avoid the river road in the morning because of the shelling!"

At that moment a shell landed just beyond the abbey and shook the earth.

Dierot angrily shook his fist at the sky, "Let he who is without sin cast the first shell!"

Then turning cheerfully to Rennaut, "Yes, Lieutenant, and each time I make it through, I keep telling you that it's the only way the horse knows. What? You seem somehow disappointed that an old man can defy the Kaiser! It gets my blood up, I guess. Well, I'll take the long road the next time I see you in confession, Rennaut. Now get me some coffee, I have some serious business to discuss."

Father Dierot—a thin, balding man with tenting eyebrows and deep vertical fissures along his cheeks—looked decidedly younger than his sixty-seven years. He walked slowly and deliberately toward the field command tent and Captain Hassan. Finding only an aide peering over torn maps at a small canvas table, he turned around to see Rennaut with a tin cup of steaming coffee lifting up the tent flap.

"Now look here, Lieutenant. I've just come from the field hospital. There were six wounded from your battalion yesterday, one seriously. And they are just boys, barely sixteen or seventeen by my reckoning. Now, I know you don't personally recruit them from North Africa or wherever they're from, but what is to be done about this? And this al-Douri boy, he may even lose his leg."

As the aide excused himself, Rennaut sat down on a tattered cloth-covered chair. In a slow and resigned voice, Rennaut began, "You are right, Father. They are just boys. Just boys. And I need men, trained men to fight. We have less than two-thirds of the soldiers left in the battalion. Almost no replacements in months. The few they sent me could barely lift a rifle, let alone fire it. All I can do is keep the boys out of the trenches and in the rear. But I don't control where the German shells go, Father. A stray shell that hit the ammunition cache a quarter mile from the front wounded those boys. With their long-range artillery, I could move our ammunition almost to Paris and they could hit it. The boys survived at least, four others yesterday didn't."

Dierot leaned forward delicately in his chair and said in a low voice, "And what of these rumors of mutiny, Rennaut? There are some villagers in Merton saying that de Clairant's men have refused to go into the trenches. Is it true? Who will defend us then?"

Rennaut did not speak at first, but then began haltingly, "It appears that some soldiers of the 67th—we don't know as yet how many—may have mutinied last night. When Captain Hassan gets back from his meeting with Captain de Clairant we will have a clearer picture. Father, the men of the Troisième are here to defend you." Rennaut said with more hope than conviction.

Dierot waited but then broke the silence and spoke with his hands clasping his face, "There was a time when Napoleon's army was the most feared and courageous in the world. I find it curious, Rennaut, that our own French soldiers fighting on their French own soil would mutiny and refuse to defend us, and yet these Arab boys are our only hope."

"I cannot speak for the other battalions, Father. But I know these men will fight the best they can."

With his hands still clasped together, Dierot slowly got up and said as he left, "I pray you are right, Rennaut. I have a christening to attend to. Perhaps I will stop by this evening on my way back. There are still a few more points to discuss."

Rennaut sat alone in the tent for a moment. He sensed that today would be the most challenging day he had faced in the army. If the Troisième did mutiny, all the efforts he had made and the risks he had taken could prove that nothing truly did matter in this or any other war. Although he believed today would be difficult, most of all, Rennaut believed in his commanding officer, Captain Michel Hassan.

CHAPTER 6

▼

Rennaut strode purposively toward the communications tent beyond the second line of trenches. He had just heard from the men that Sergeant Mahmoud had returned from the night patrol with several German prisoners. A dark skinned private with a red cloth hat saluted and lifted back the tent flap for Rennaut. He remarked as he entered, "Well done, Sergeant." As he shook Mahmoud's hand, he noticed a bloodstained bandage around his upper arm and remarked, "Any wounded on the patrol?"

"Nothing serious, sir," he replied. "Just more uncut wire than we expected."

Seated in the center of the tent were two sorry German soldiers slumped in makeshift chairs. Rennaut gazed at the two despondent figures, their gray coats covered in mud and thought, "My God, the Germans are down to the same old men and boys that we are."

"Sergeant Mahmoud, have you removed everything relevant from their belongings?"

"Yes, Lieutenant Rennaut."

"Very well then. Take them to the mess tent and get them something to eat." Rennaut stared at the Germans' insignias on their shoulders. Both had the familiar black and gold eagle of the 98th Bavarian Infantry. "And Sergeant, clean them up. We don't want to send them back to the Kaiser looking second rate for the Saturday night dance."

Informal prisoner exchanges at the front, common in the first year of the war, were now expressly forbidden by the High Command. The underutilized and bored intelligence officers at Lefevre's headquarters liked nothing more than to practice their German on the prisoners and draw sweeping conclusions from the slightest bit of indirect evidence. On Hassan's tacit orders, however, the German prisoners never made it to Lefevre's headquarters and were exchanged for captured French soldiers after forty-eight hours of minimal questioning. The German commander reluctantly reciprocated, although his practice was to hold captives for seventy-two hours just to prove a point.

Rennaut turned then to Sergeant Mahmoud, "And go to the dressing station and have that wound cleaned properly."

"Yes, Lieutenant. Sir, you may wish to look at these things first," Mahmoud said as he handed Rennaut a small canvas bag. The bag held the personal effects of the two prisoners. As Rennaut spread its contents on the table, two things immediately startled him among the usual collage of letters, pictures, field maps, watches, and requisite small Bibles. There was a small crust of black bread that, on inspection, was so soft it must have been freshly baked. Most importantly, there were two bank notes that were unmistakably Russian rubles. Rennaut turned to the private manning the telegraph wire and looked at is watch. It was nearly eight o'clock. "Hassan will have just reached the 67th by now," he thought.

As the prisoners were led from the tent, Rennaut hurriedly scratched out a note and handed it to the private, "Send this immediately to Captain Hassan at de Clairant's headquarters."

NIGHT PATROL SUCCESSFUL. STOP. REASON TO BELIEVE FROM CAPTURED TROOPS THAT GERMANS WILL ATTACK IN 24 HOURS. STOP. RENNAUT.

Shortly after breakfast, Captain Michel Hassan and his aide, Corporal Leconde, began the two-mile journey on horseback to the headquarters of the 67th infantry battalion. Hassan stopped at the edge of the village to quickly sketch the abbey in the distance and then proceeded to take the ancient stone road to the east. After a quarter-mile outside of town, they began to encounter men in groups of threes and fours sitting in the tall grass beside the road talking idly. Some still had their rifles, Hassan observed, but most did not. Seeing the gold captain's bars, a few soldiers stood and saluted as the two men rode by. Most, however, were indifferent, preferring not to recognize the trappings of an army they despised.

As they approached de Clairant's headquarters in an abandoned schoolhouse outside the village of Merton there was surprisingly little activity. The two men dismounted and entered a darkened hallway; only the smell of tobacco and coffee suggested human activity. Hassan walked past the rows of empty school desks and peered at two figures staring out the window. It was de Clairant and an aide manning a telegraph station.

"Alex, is that you?"

"Michel, you're here. Michel, I'm so glad to see you. You see, they've all gone! They wouldn't listen to me or the other officers. They've all gone." He kept repeating to himself as he sank into the chair.

Captain Alex de Clairant had the aristocratic credentials, but not the demeanor to be a leader of men. Had he not been Colonel Lefevre's nephew, it would have been highly unlikely that he would have commanded a battalion. Short and wiry, his receding hair made him look somewhat older than his thirty-two years. He had loved his university studies in linguistics and the café life surrounding L'Ecole Normale Superieure. The thought of a military career was just something to transiently please his father, who, after all, paid the bills. The military academy at St-Cyr could take years to finish and the war would be over by then. Or so they all said. However, when the army reduced officers' compulsory training from three years to fourteen months the equation looked quite different. Little in Alex de Clairant's military training at St-Cyr or the long weekends at the chateau with his uncle's society friends had prepared him for a full-scale mutiny. In fact, little he learned had any relevance at all to trench warfare or defensive fighting whatsoever. Only the classic methods of attack were appropriate subjects for the French army. In his two months at the head of the decimated 67th battalion, he had never even discussed a plan for the attack.

Hassan sat next to de Clairant, looked directly at his face hidden in his trembling hands and asked, deliberately, "Alex, listen to me. Where are the other officers and Sergeant Nevers?" Hassan had known the reputation of Nevers and knew the tough old salt, like Rennaut, would never mutiny or desert.

"Nevers took a small detail, I think, and went to secure the sentry post in front of the communications trench. I think Breton and Meyes went to try to talk to the men by the road or perhaps by the train station. But it's no use—they won't listen to anyone."

Just then the telegraph clerk ripped off his earpiece and blurted excitedly, "Captain Hassan, this message just came for you!"

Hassan read aloud the telegraphed message from Rennaut and then sat down in the chair next to de Clairant and was silent for a moment. He then stood up and spoke clearly and firmly, "Leconde, go to the communications trench and find Sergeant Nevers. Have him report back here immediately. Then ride back to our headquarters and tell Rennaut to have the men assemble after stand-in. He then peered at the long slate blackboard and turned to speak to de Clairant,

"Alex, the first thing I want you to do is to send Nevers on horseback to contact Captain Legrange. Have him tell Legrange to immediately move up all his artillery batteries and ammunition reserves to support your position. Nevers is to tell him that it's an order from headquarters."

De Clairant mildly protested, "But isn't that a decision for the Colonel?"

Hassan leaned over and responded calmly, "You let me worry about your uncle, Alex. Unless those artillery batteries move up tonight there won't be a regiment tomorrow for Lefevre to inspect." Then turning to the blackboard and handing a piece of chalk to de Clairant, he said, "Now the second thing: I want you to draw for me the location of your machine gun positions in your first two trenches."

De Clairant looked down at a series of maps on the telegraph table. He then strode to the blackboard and drew three parallel lines and slowly filled in his six machine gun positions marking them with an X.

At just that moment Lieutenant Meyes burst into the headquarters and excitedly proclaimed, "The Senegalese, sir, the rifle company, sir; they are with us, they are back in the trenches!"

The moment of unspoken good fortune was tempered with irony as the four men reflected on this sudden piece of news. A single company of black Senegalese riflemen was all that could be counted on from the mutinous 67th French battalion. Once the most feared and professional army in all Europe, the pride of Napoleon and the Empire, was now solely dependent on its African territorials.

Hassan spoke directly to Lieutenant Meyes while writing on the board, "When Sergeant Nevers comes back, you will divide the company of Senegalese in half. Nevers will take half the men and set up machine positions on the flanks of the second-line trenches here and here. You will take the other half of the company and position your men here, in the center, also in the second-line trench. Abandon the frontline trenches and remove all the ammunition to the second line. The first line will be destroyed in the barrage anyway. Everyone must stay below in the dugouts until after the barrage is over and then quickly set up the machine guns. I will send a company from my battalion this afternoon to reinforce your center. Your Enfields in the center will occupy the Germans just coming out of the first-line trenches. You must set up intersecting fields of fire on the flanks with your machine guns."

Then turning to de Clairant he spoke firmly, "Alex, you must take charge and coordinate with the artillery. You must mass the artillery in the center behind the third trench line, but do not under any circumstances let Legrange's batteries open up too early and give away their positions. You must wait until after the

Germans have committed their reserves. They will be the ones with the fresh uniforms and shiny helmets. Do you understand? When the German reserves come out of the first-line trenches, give the signal to Legrange to open up with every seventy-five he's got. You must tell Legrange that the initial fire must be directed solely against the reserve units, not the attacking force of the Bavarians. The reserves must not reinforce the assault and break though in the center. Is that clear? When everything is in place, I will telegraph Gastineau and Lefevre with our plan. Once they have countersigned it, I will inform you all by courier." The three men nodded and left the room.

At 8:20, Rennaut detected in his field glasses a lone rider approaching from the eastern road. He knew the characteristic canter of the horse and had the bugler sound the call for assembly. Within minutes the men of the 3d Moroccan formed into five straight lines, rifles at the ready. Hassan hurriedly dismounted, brushed off his tunic, and nodded to Rennaut. He scanned the taut faces of boys who in a few short months at Valcourt had become men and the old veterans who had helped them survive. He walked with a calm resolve and knew what he had to say. The truth in simple terms was what was required.

Hassan stood upon a small mound in the parade area and addressed the troops. He began slowly and confidently, "Men of the Troisième, the rumors that you have heard about a mutiny are true. I have just come from Captain de Clairant's headquarters and some men under his command have left the trenches. The Senegalese riflemen, however, are there and are dug in for the coming fight." Murmurs went through the lines and Hassan briefly paused.

He then resumed, "I cannot speak for the High Command. I cannot guess what they will do, but any man in this battalion who is not prepared to fight can drop his weapon, step forward, and leave now with no reprisal from me. Those who stay must be prepared for the coming battle. This battalion holds the British flank. I don't need to tell you that if the Germans break through here, they will wipe out the English. The men that stay and fight with me will bring honor to themselves and the distinguished service of this territorial battalion."

Hassan waited for a moment, his head scanning the five long lines of men with rifles at the ready. No one moved. Not a single man stepped forward. He then saluted Rennaut, turned, and walked to the staff headquarters. Rennaut walked to the head of the battalion and scanned the lines of the men, rigid and unmoving at attention. Rennaut's voice wavered with emotion for an instant in a barely perceptible way as he shouted, "Dis-missed! Officers report to staff."

Rennaut and the other lieutenants in charge of their companies walked together to the staff tent. Seeing Hassan seated at the map table, he put his arm on Michel's shoulder and said, "By God these boys will fight, sir. God help the Kaiser tomorrow."

"Yes, Rennaut, but I'd like the our chances better with an artillery battalion backing us up all the same. I've shifted them all to de Clairant. He's in a bad way, but with any luck we'll draw the main attack here against us. Sit down. I've been thinking about our plan. The train station and truck depot that we defend, gentlemen, are the Germans' main objectives. They know the Brits are going to attack soon when the mud dries up for their tanks. If they capture this village, we cannot resupply the British offensive and the Brits face the real possibility of being flanked. However, their main artillery barrage, I'm guessing will be directed not at us, but at de Clairant to try drawing away some of our strength for the main infantry attack against us. They know we are undermanned, but we have the high ground here. We will send Second Company to de Clairant to shore up his center. Each man must take a Lee Enfield with him and as many bullet clips as he can carry. I've told de Clairant to take Legrange's entire artillery battalion and mass it in the center to support his defense, so we will not have them to back us up. We will not defend the first trenches line; Fourth and Fifth companies will set up along the ridgeline in the second and third set of third trenches. Riflemen will be in the second trenches and machine gunners only in the third. I want the all machine guns positioned on our flanks. As soon as the Germans capture the first trench line, the riflemen in the second trenches will retreat on my command to the third-line trenches. Let's hope that as soon as the German command sees our riflemen retreat to our third line they will commit their entire reserves to the center and stop their rolling barrage."

Rennaut then interrupted, "But sir, what about First and Third companies?"

"Rennaut, you and Lieutenant Mustaf will take both your companies tonight to hide in the marshes beyond the river. You will be in command, Rennaut. After they commit their reserves, I will signal you to counterattack on their flank. No one knows that area better than you, and you will show the men where best to cross the river. You will take extra ammunition and all the grenades you can carry. You must stay there out of sight during the barrage. I know that will be difficult, but there is no other way. I will fire a flare when I see their reserves go into action and start to occupy the first trench line. At that moment, you will counterattack with First and Third companies from the river marsh. They will not be suspecting an attack from the river. Hopefully, you will catch their reserves in the first trench line. Any questions?"

Rennaut inquired plaintively, "Clear enough, sir. But does this mean, sir, we can double the wine rations?" The Muslim lieutenants just smiled as they left the tent.

That afternoon Lefevre reached Hassan on the telephone. The Colonel feared it was too risky to travel to the front. When Hassan explained the situation and his general plans for coordinating the defenses, Lefevre said, as he patted his moustache after finishing his tea, "Suitable, suitable."

That night, Hassan sent word for Rennaut to meet him at his field tent before crossing the river. Rennaut entered shortly after 10:00, after checking on the other men and company commanders. Hassan poured him a glass of cognac into a tin cup.

"It seems like the right time for the good stuff, sir," said Rennaut.

"Good luck tomorrow, Allain."

"The boys will do fine, sir. It's the 67th I'm worried about. But with all the regiment's artillery, I suspect they'll have a chance, sir."

"Well, I hope I'm right on this gamble. Anyway, Allain, I want to ask you to do a favor for me."

"Certainly, sir."

"Allain, depending on what happens tomorrow, I would like you to post these letters for me." Then reaching for a canvas leaning against the table, he said, "And one other thing, I would like you to take this portrait to Robine's widow in Le Havre. After the severe burns I don't think she could recognize his body. I wanted her to have a different memory of him. You can wrap the painting in this burlap here."

Rennaut was transfixed by the likeness of Robine with his blue officer's tunic emerging from the shadows of the abbey in afternoon light.

"It's remarkable, sir. It's just as if he were walking up to me for morning report. There's even that small scar on his cheek, sir, and his sunburned nose. Well, I'd be very proud to give this to the widow, sir. Excepting the circumstances. He was good man and he loved the boys."

"Yes, he was a fine man and a fine officer."

"Excuse me, sir, the rumor is, well, that it was one of those stray gas shells that killed him. Was it, sir, just a stray shell?"

"Yes, Rennaut. Just a stray shell. Does it matter?" Hassan replied.

Rennaut did not quickly respond, but then began, "Like the stray one that hit al-Douri and those boys from Tangiers. The thing is, sir, I sent them that afternoon to round up firewood away from the front because I thought it was too dangerous here. Too dangerous here." Rennaut's voice trailed off as he sipped from the tin cup.

Rennaut then continued, "You see, sir, the boys keep asking me how it's all going to end. And I keep telling them what I'm sure of: it'll end when all the soldiers on both sides are dead. That's how. But what I can't for the life of me figure out is how this all happened to begin with. Can you, sir? I mean the Brits and Russians are our natural enemies. Now they're both our allies. Sure we've had a few rows with the Germans before, but I mean, what do we have against the Austrians, or for the Turks for that matter? And what do the Germans have against our Arab boys or the Senegalese?"

Hassan could only shake his head. After a while he spoke again, "Oh, and one more thing Allain. I know how much the men rely on you. I want you to know how much I rely on you. I know that the show of support by the men today was as much your doing as anyone's and I thank you. Now I think I'll check on the men."

The two men put their hands on each others' shoulders and withdrew into their private thoughts. As Rennaut gathered a few last reports and maps to take back to his dugout to study, he saw through the yellowish filter of the canvas tent a kerosene lamp weave back and forth. He knew within moments he would hear the plaintive voice of Father Dierot.

"Is your dance card quite full, Lieutenant?" asked Dierot as he pulled back the flap and walked to center of the tent. Observing the bottle of cognac, he offered, "Well, let's try some of the local produce, shall we?" and placed a bottle of peach brandy on the table.

"Good evening, Father. If I were to hazard a guess, I'd imagine that you might be inquiring about the events in de Clairant's sector."

"A good guess, but not really, Rennaut. You see, I stopped in town on my way back and, by the look of the number of de Clairant's men milling about the train station, the situation is pretty clear. We'll be depending on you alone to hold off the Germans. Mind you, the Boche are not all that bad. I still remember our last war with them forty years ago. Now that was a fine war. All over in a few big dustups. The Germans had the satisfaction of booting us out of Paris, but did they really want to occupy us and give up their sausages and beer for red wine and smelly cheese? No, of course not. Well, I for one, Rennaut, have had enough of the war for a moment. I view this as more of a social chat," he replied while pouring the drinks.

Dierot continued, "You see, I've gotten to know the commanders of this part of the line pretty well over the past two years. Hassan and Robine before him.

Damn fine men. Decent men. But you, Rennaut, have eluded me thus far. You've been too preoccupied with military matters it seems. So Hassan's the man I deal with mostly. He'll tell you the truth at least. Cares about the men. Hard for me to imagine a good man like that killing anybody, but that's a foreign concept to an old cleric like me anyway. I suspect you're a bit like me some ways, an outsider. Imagine going to grade school in these parts with an English mother!"

After an awkward silence Rennaut offered, "What did you wish to speak about father?"

Dierot turned around as he got up to leave, "Only to wish you luck, my son. You see, the villagers feel and I quite agree that you are defending a sacred place. The abbey and the windows. That's all, my son."

CHAPTER 7

▼

The Germans, if nothing else, were a comfort in their predictability. The thunderous crash of their general barrage began the next morning precisely at thirty minutes after 8:00. For the men of the Troisième deep underground, the tremulous earthen walls of their dugouts shook loose bits of clods as reminders of the destruction above. The rolling barrage against the barbed wire began an hour later. It was heaviest first in de Clairant's sector, as Hassan had predicted; by 9:30, the wire in no-man's-land and the first trench lines were no longer recognizable, just random piles of mud and debris. Except for Hassan in the sentry post beneath the abbey and four other posted sentries above the dugouts, all the men stayed below in their deep underground bunkers along the second and third trench lines. Hassan scanned with his field glasses along the river, but Rennaut and his men were completely hidden in the willows. The barrage seemed to slightly decrease in intensity, and at 9:40 AM, Hassan saw flashes of light reflected off the Germans' spiked helmets as they bobbed in and out of the bomb craters in no-man's-land. Soon the brown landscape turned to gray, with the swarming mass of three full German infantry battalions. Having some 1,000 yards to cover before they reached the undefended first trench line, Hassan calculated that it would take the crack Germans assault troops eight minutes with full battle gear. On their extreme right flank, he could just make out what appeared to be another infantry battalion heading across the desolate terrain toward de Clairant's lines.

Hassan had not heard Legrange's artillery battalion open up yet and said to himself, "Wait just a little longer. Wait for the reserves. Don't give your positions away yet."

Hassan then blew his officer's whistle and in rapid succession the other sentries blew theirs. He ran to the closest of the five dugouts and shouted the order, "Take your trench positions! Riflemen in the second and machine gunners in the third! Riflemen hold your fire until you hear my command. Snipers only shoot at the officers. The ones with the plumes on the helmets. Wait until they've cleared the first trench line. Pass the order." The men quickly scrambled out of their dugouts to their assigned posts with the machine gunners setting up the tripods and ammunition clips and the snipers adjusting the scopes on their sights.

Hassan followed with his binoculars the lead attacking group. Despite the mass of uniforms, he soon could make out clearly a single officer's plumed helmet. With his right arm violently waving a Luger, the German lieutenant urged his men forward to quickly reach the shelter of the first trench line. Over the undulating and scarred terrain, Hassan saw the helmet appear and then disappear over the next 100 yards. As he approached within a dozen yards of the first trench line the officer turned to face his men with pistol held high and then swung round to lead the attack. At that moment, Hassan saw in his field glasses a sniper's bullet explode through the German lieutenant's neck. Blood spurted from his mouth as the force jerked him violently backward. Hassan saw his blue eyes open wide with terror, then close. The German then fell backward to the ground spread-eagle, as his pistol fired a shot aimlessly upward into the thin blue smoke still hovering from the barrage.

Still the sea of gray uniforms continued forward and forward. Within moments the German vanguard reached the first trench line barely 200 yards away. Rennaut and his men sequestered among the willows were stretched out in three columns in the firmer earth above the bank sloping toward the river. Rennaut took off his blue tunic and climbed the tallest tree with his field glasses. It was both frightening and exhilarating to see the enormous size of the German force slowly winding his way up the long incline towards the abbey. "This is it." He thought. "They've gambled it all." Rennaut marveled at the discipline of the machine gunners of the Troisième, who held their fire despite the easy targets. He then caught site of several German battalion flags furling their gold and black standards as they entered the French frontline trenches. "It won't be long now boys," Rennaut said to himself.

With the apparent success of the Germans in capturing the French frontline trenches, Hassan saw in his binoculars another wave of German infantry jumping off from their forward lines, "That must be their reserves," he said to himself. He abruptly fired a flare as a signal to Rennaut and then waited for several excruciating minutes as the German shock troops scrambled up and over the captured first trench with their reserves now only 200 yards behind rushing to reinforce the attack. Turning to his men Hassan shouted, "Fire!" The intersecting bursts of fire from the Lee Enfields cut down the German rows like harvesting gray sheaves of wheat. The riflemen in the second line furiously blasted away at anyone leading a salient of troops. As soon as the front rows of Germans fell, others quickly took their place stepping over shattered dead and wounded. Hassan knew that many brave men had already died in this assault, but, owing to the sheer numbers of the Germans, his machine gunners held in reserve in the third trench would run out of ammunition unless Rennaut's flanking attack was successful.

Hassan could see that as quickly as one row of Germans was knocked down another took its place, but now in groups of five or eight, not fifteen or twenty. Hassan again furiously blew his whistle sounding the retreat for the riflemen who hurled their last grenades down the slopes and exited along the sides of the trenches for the safety of the third line.

Rennaut had seen the flare and descended from the tree. He quickly gave the order for the companies to move out. "Listen to me, men, don't throw your grenades into the trenches until I give the hand signal."

Rennaut and Mustaf led the two lines of men as they crawled, grenades in hand, 100 feet behind the captured first trench that held the German reserves. Rifles with fixed bayonets slung behind their backs, the nimble men of the Troisième held grenades in both hands as they furiously slithered along propelled only by elbows and knees. The short brown grass was still damp with dew and the earth smelled foul from the combination of gunpowder and decaying black leaves.

Rennaut decided he would not just attack the right flank of the enemy; he would attack it directly from the rear by crawling with his troops as far behind the German reserves in the trench as possible. They slowly kept crawling amid the explosions and cries of the battle. The next few anxious minutes seemed to last forever until all 100 men got into position. The German reserves were fixated by the firefight directly ahead of them as the two French companies slowly took up their positions unnoticed behind them and coalesced into a single long line with Mustaf on the left, Rennaut on the right.

The German regimental commanding officer, Colonel Karl von Veitz scanned the field with his high-powered telescope from a newly erected observation platform he had specially constructed for the battle. He could not believe the horror of the scene unfolding directly before him. Von Veitz could clearly see Rennaut's troops crawling behind his German soldiers but was powerless to inform his men.

He visualized in a dreamlike state of slow motion the destruction of a battalion of his finest reserve troops, the Prussian 109th battalion, led by Prince Ultmeyer.

He watched helplessly in terror as Rennaut raised his arm high and pumped his fist twice. A hundred men of the Troisième then released two grenades in rapid succession into the trench of the unsuspecting German reserves. The ground heaved with wooden fragments, helmets, dirt, and shards of shattered bodies rising up into the smoky air. The distance muffled the sounds of the grenade blasts and the screams of disintegrating men. Von Veitz could only see the slaughter of the few individual men who were able to climb out of the trench and were immediately cut down. When the blast subsided, the Troisième rushed to the edge of the trench and blew apart point blank with their rifles the few remaining enemy still capable of moving.

"Bayonets!" Rennaut screamed as the Moroccans leaped into the trench and hacked away at the wounded and already dead. When the bloodletting had finished Rennaut shouted, "Up the hill!"

Officers leading the first wave of the German shock troops advancing up the slope toward the abbey suddenly realized that they were now being attacked from the rear. Rifle fire and bayonets from Rennaut's men cut down scores of troops in the back. Some German officers tried to order a retreat, but they turned directly into Rennaut's line of steady fire.

Von Veitz was now faced with not just the loss of two reserve battalions, but with his entire regiment. His troops attacking de Clairant were completely neutralized by the massed French artillery that shattered the advancing German reserves in no-man's-land. The French artillery had waited until the last moment to avoid giving away their positions to the German artillery. Now von Veitz foresaw his entire army destroyed by a much smaller French force that had outsmarted him and laid to waist his crack German battalions. He struggled to overcome his panic and then ordered his personal company of Royal Guards into the battle. Von Veitz then commanded his artillery officer Captain Franz Schulnitz to fire on his own men now fighting hand to hand with Rennaut's two companies. Schulnitz refused to fire on German troops and cursed the "Prussian madman!" Von Veitz immediately had his guards arrest him, and they wrestled him screaming to the rear.

Hassan was shocked by the blast of the first German artillery rounds falling directly on Rennaut's men locked together with the German troops. He saw with his binoculars Allain thrown up in the air by an artillery burst, but moments later start to crawl away. A Moroccan soldier ran up to Rennaut and dragged him by the shoulder back to the first trench line, but a bullet cut down the soldier just as he threw Rennaut into the trench. Many of the Troisième retreated to the trench, but others were blown up in the artillery blasts. Hassan through his binoculars now saw the black helmets of the company of 250 German Royal Guards approaching the first trench line. Although seemingly transfixed, he suddenly became aware of a man pulling furiously on his arm and shouting in his ear. It was a man he did not recognize, but he saw his artillery insignia.

The man shouted in his ear, "Sir, I'm Sergeant Mouton from the 119th artillery. Sergeant Nevers sent me to help you out. I brought some artillery to see if you needed any help, sir."

Hassan turned around and saw on the road beside the abbey twenty-mule teams dragging French 75-mm guns and a Fiat truck with ammunition.

"But what of Legrange and the attack on de Clairant?"

Sergeant Mouton continued to shout above the din, "de Clairant and Legrange were killed, sir. Nevers took command. But we routed them, sir, we put all our artillery up against their reserves and they ran sir, they ran! The Germans ran!"

Hassan pointed as he shouted back, "Set up your guns right here. Right here all together in a row. Fire directly right at those men attacking our first trench line. Do you see them? The Germans with the black helmets there! Fire at them, fire immediately!"

Within minutes the first French shells fell sporadically among the onrushing Royal Guards and now too the French machine guns held in reserve began to open up. Michel fixed his glasses on the German company commander holding the banner of his colors high as he raced to the trench line seemingly impervious to the shelling and machine gun fire. Instants later, bursting shells landed directly on the commander and the advancing Germans, flinging fragments of twenty shattered bodies high into the air. The Guards were stunned and stopped their advance as the machine gun fire from the flanks intensified. Without their commander, the men panicked and retreated.

Three Moroccans from Rennaut's company spontaneously jumped out of the first line trench and charged after the retreating Royal Guards firing as they went, shooting them in the back with clips from their Enfields. Still the Germans continued to shell their own troops fighting in close combat as they retreated from the abbey. As Hassan looked around the exploding shell bursts near the second trench line, a thin black figure was walking slowly between the dead and dying. He fixed his glasses upon him and saw Father Dierot kneeling down to give last rites to all the fallen in his path, French and German alike.

"No!" Hassan cried. He leapt from the sentry post and raced toward Dierot with shells bursting on all sides. He tackled Dierot to the ground and began to drag him to the second trench as a concussion shell threw them both into the air and into the trench. Mansour, close behind, lifted Hassan onto his shoulder and put his right arm around the priest and dragged them both toward the dugout at the end of the trench.

The three Moroccan riflemen continued to zigzag across no-man's-land as they charged the few remaining retreating Royal Guards. They did not stop as they shot them in the legs and back and bayoneted them as they stumbled toward the forward German trenches. Several German officers tripped over fallen bodies as they retreated, and the Moroccans bayoneted them through the abdomen in a single violent thrust and kept on moving. Von Veitz screamed at his bodyguards to immediately open fire at the Moroccans, thus killing several retreating Germans in the mayhem. Enraged, he quickly got down from his platform, then mounted his horse, and moved down a small embankment to the front German trench to personally direct the fire. German snipers surrounding the general cut down a first and then a second Moroccan. The final Moroccan now raced directly up a small knoll toward the high command, not stopping to fire until he saw the oversized man on horseback with his gleaming sliver helmet with red plumes. The small brown-skinned man stood erect with his red kepi cap visible to all amid a mass of gray bodies. The Moroccan slowly and deliberately lifted his Enfield in a swirling hail of machinegun bullets. He squeezed off a single round, piercing the general's monocle. It burst through the back of his skull, jolting his lifeless frame to the earth.

The last German shell, fired in anger at their crushing defeat, landed directly on Hassan's dugout as Mansour's body sheltered both him and Dierot.

PART II

CHAPTER 8

▼

A single stand of gently bending poplars broke the plane between earth and sky across the broad expanse of wheat fields ringing the tiny chapel at Courville. Tradition held that twelfth-century stonemasons, glaziers, and laborers erecting the great cathedral at Chartres built the small chapel as a place to worship during the long decades of construction. The chapel's architectural design, however, was atypical for the late medieval period. Less formal and imposing in style, it nevertheless required exceptional engineering and aesthetic skill to harmonize the oversized windows with its diminutive structure. Yet for the men and women who worshipped there daily, the most compelling attribute of the small chapel was its sense of spiritual intimacy. Chartres, with its spires and vaulted ceilings reaching to the heavens, was built on an almost unfathomable scale. Its otherworldly dimensions created in the minds of some villagers an uneasy sense of distance. The chapel at Courville, despite its intricate stonework and vivid stained glass windows, was approachable to its parishioners and on the scale they could understand. Over the years, many who worked on the construction of the cathedral asked to be buried near the chapel, and a small village grew up around it. In 1867 an orphanage was erected adjacent to the small chapel by the church fathers in Chartres, thereby bringing a sense of vibrancy and renewal to this ancient spiritual center.

By the time Michel Hassan was four and able to attend the orphanage at Courville, there was much speculation among the nuns about his family origins. Some thought his father had been an Algerian officer in the French army or a wealthy Tunisian merchant. Others felt certain he was the son of a Moroccan sheik. There was, however, no doubt that the mother had been French, as Michel was clearly identified as "mixed race" on his entrance forms. When both parents died of cholera, baby Michel was sent with a servant from North Africa to live with his aunt in the small village of Thivars, seven kilometers from Chartres. His aunt died in a fire that burned down the main house that same year. Michel was sleeping with his wet nurse in a stone cottage near the estate and was saved from the fire. His small inheritance made possible admission to the orphanage at Courville rather than being transported to the large custodial institutions for the poor in Paris.

Michel was one of the relatively few younger boys at the orphanage. After all, boys could grow up to become laborers or apprentices and were deemed by surviving relatives to be much more economically desirable than girls. There were no dowries to finance, no honor to uphold, and no tedious courtship rituals. There were plenty of older boys at the orphanage aged eight to twelve who had proved themselves to be lazy or shiftless, but at age three or four, boys were prized as potential workers among the local farmers and merchants. In fact, Michel's very first memories of the orphanage reflected this somewhat elevated status as the nuns fussed over his dressing and feeding. Nursery rhymes, stray dogs lying in the shadows of the courtyard, and limitless open fields filled the thoughts of the small child. Although with time he became conscious that the village boys and girls had parents and he did not, Michel nevertheless, felt a certain measure of love and acceptance within his surroundings.

This sentiment changed abruptly when, at the age of six, Michel entered the orphanage school. It was the first time he encountered social and racial prejudice among the older children, expressed in muffled slurs or minor incidents of ostracism on the playground. When Michel excelled in his studies, jealousy was added to this volatile mixture. Michel was a loner, and the older boys, sensing weakness, began to gang up and attack him in packs of three or four. A call to action to deal with these distressing skirmishes came from an unlikely source, the school nurse. When Michel presented himself to Sister Helene at the infirmary with multiple scrapes and bruises, he was surprised by her outward lack of sympathy.

Sister Helene offered little comfort and remarked in a rather offhand way while rubbing his bruises with witch hazel, "My child, you will have to learn this old truth eventually, God helps those who help themselves."

That night Michel pondered the meaning of Sister Helene's remark. The dawning recognition that he alone was going to have to deal with this problem was agonizing at first, but in the end proved liberating. Michel plotted his revenge by first arming himself with a fist-sized rock and a broken-off broom handle that he carried hidden in his cloth school bag. When next attacked by the mob, he immediately took on the largest of his assailants with the rock and then chased off the others with his improvised club. He knew, however, that over time these purely defensive measures would be insufficient. Michel carefully studied the habits and characteristic routes of his individual foes. One by one he picked them off at the time and place of his choosing. No polite rules of engagement operated here and he jumped out at them from behind doorways or fences and beat them with the same ferocity they had shown him. Then he would drag them out into the courtyard by their hair where all the children, especially the girls, would see his attacker, in a public display, beg for mercy. He gave no quarter in the process and Sister Helene said nothing to her superiors about the mounting casualties piling up at the infirmary.

Michel had not planned to end his campaign until all of his tormentors had been both physically and psychologically humiliated. After the two older bullies, Henri and Jean-Luc had been subdued, only the last remained, a smaller nine-year-old boy named Claude. Claude specialized in profanity and racial taunts from the relative safety of the protection of the larger boys.

In the midst of thrashing Claude in the dirt courtyard one Saturday afternoon, a blurry figure suddenly darted from the shadows out at the combatants. The whirlwind interloper repeatedly struck Michel with surprising intensity shouting, "Stop it! Stop it right now!"

Michel immediately turned to face the intruder. He was startled to find that the commanding voice originated from a small girl. He felt ashamed, even dirty. He walked away with no satisfaction, only the newfound guilt as an aggressor.

Michel learned that her name was Camille and on several occasions over the next three months he sought her after school to apologize and make her understand his reasons for the attacks. She rebuffed him at every turn, refusing to talk to him at first and then shouting back at him, "You're just as bad as they are!" As the rejections became more painful, Michel withdrew and spoke to fewer and fewer people, feeling mistrusted and alone. He had assumed the responsibility for his own protection and safety, but the solution itself entailed violence and humiliation in the process; the same tactics of his foes.

Sadly, Camille Richard was no stranger to violence. Her mother had abruptly abandoned her family when she turned two and her father openly blamed Camille for it. He died crashing down the cellar steps in an alcoholic rage, ending years of neglect and abuse. Fortunately, he had not had time to change his will before he died. The proceeds of the sale of their house enabled Camille to attend the orphanage at Courville. Thinner than most, with spindly legs and brown bangs that nearly covered her green eyes, Camille took great comfort in the regimentation of the orphanage, with its fixed time for meals, school, and prayers. Her bed in the dormitory was always neatly made and her white blouse and navy blue skirt always meticulously hung on the hook beside her nightstand. Despite her love for order and discipline, Camille was at heart a libertarian, willing to question many of the seemingly arcane orphanage rules that had evolved arbitrarily over many decades.

Camille discovered during chapel and singing hymns with the nuns that she possessed a passion for music. She began to embark on a great campaign that would preoccupy her for the next several years, namely to gain admission to the orphanage choir. Although girls outnumbered boys roughly two to one, there was only a single orphanage choir and it was composed entirely of boys. The twenty carefully chosen choirboys practiced twice weekly in the orphanage chapel and also on Tuesday and Saturday afternoons in the church in Courville with its fine organ. Saturday was market day and if Monsieur Elluard the choirmaster, felt the rehearsal went well enough he bought small candy treats for the boys. In addition to regular performances in Courville, twice a year the boy's choir went on trips, once during Christmas holidays to perform at Chartres cathedral and in the spring a trip to Paris to perform for the bishop at his opulent residence.

On Mondays and Wednesdays, Camille would dutifully sit in the back of the chapel listening to the rehearsals and memorizing each solo part. When it was over, she would dash to a vacant classroom on the third floor that had a small upright piano to practice her scales for an hour. She would then rehearse the parts to all the songs for a second hour. Only the elderly blue Siamese cat that slept on the window ledge in the afternoon sunshine had the benefit of her remarkable voice. On numerous occasions, she had pleaded her case to Mr. Elluard and Sister Monique to be allowed to join the choir. There polite answers were always variations of the same response, "That is why it is called the Boy's Choir, my dear."

In preparation for the bishop's concert, his personal secretary, Monsignor Bernarde, traveled from Paris for the final rehearsal to coordinate all the travel arrangements for the boys. The bishop had never been fond of solemn liturgical music and held the yearly concert in a grand private room in his palace in order to hear his favorite baroque arias away from the pious gaze of other less musically inclined clerics.

Within the first half-hour, it became apparent to Bernarde as he sat in the back row that the rehearsals were not going well. Unfamiliar with the music, however, he was uncertain as to the underlying problem. The harmony and rhythm seemed right, yet something was missing. He wondered to himself if the soloist was perhaps not as accomplished as he had heard in the past.

During a brief interlude in the singing, Bernarde spoke up loudly from the rear of the chapel, "If you don't mind my interrupting, choirmaster, what is the effect you are trying to achieve with the solo in this piece? It escapes me."

Deeply annoyed by this amateurish challenge, Elluard slowly turned and fixed his wrathful gaze in the general vicinity of the back of the chapel and responded, "Well, since you're obviously not familiar with this work, let me try to simplify it for you. The effect one is obviously trying to achieve in the solo is to express a tone of brightness, confidence, and exhilaration through the elaboration of the sense of precision that directly leads from the demanding castrati elements of the high notes."

"And what again exactly, if you don't mind, are the main elements of the castrati notes?" shot back Bernarde.

"The main element is, of course, the incorporation of the feminine sensibility in the vibrato and tone of the high notes. Or to put it in a more simple way that you might possibly understand, it is to have the soloist sound the high sweet notes of a girl."

At that point a clear and bright feminine voice came forth from the shadows of a side aisle, "Then, choirmaster, why not let a girl sing it in the first place?"

There was first a collective murmur and then silence at this brazen interruption. Elluard, however, soon became visibly irritated at this upstart. In his anger he took the bait, replying, "Well, young lady, let's just put an end to this nonsense once and for all. Shall we? Let's just see how well you can do this. Beginning from the second stanza."

Finally given her chance, Camille was energized with a sense of joy. She sang the entire solo flawlessly. The unanticipated power and beauty of the sound that filled the chapel was met by a period of silent disbelief. Finally, it was Bernarde who spoke, "Well, it looks to me like you've solved the soloist problem, choirmaster. I will make all the necessary arrangement for travel and lodging. This young girl can stay with Sister Marta. The bishop will adore the child."

CHAPTER 9

▼

He was known affectionately by the nuns simply as the "capuchin de la terre." True, his prominent bald spot was somewhat reminiscent of a friar's tonsure, yet it was his gentle manner that reflected a deep reverence and humility toward all natural things and an unfailing cheerfulness in the face of an ordinary life. The face was deeply lined, revealing softness when he smiled and gestured in his animated way to the nuns. Tommasso, the Sicilian gardener, had been part of the human fabric of the orphanage as long as anyone could remember.

Michel at age eight was an unusually tall, slender boy with dark chocolate eyes and wavy coal black hair. He was different from the other boys, who seemed tempestuous bundles of unfocused energy, and Michel carried himself with a noticeable pride. It is possible that he may have had some premonition of his great gift as an exceptionally talented artist. This was first noticed inadvertently by Tommasso, who lived alone in a small cottage at the edge of the orphanage property.

Perhaps it was his dark facial features, bronzed by years of work in the fields that drew him to Tommasso, but at the age of eight Michel came up to him by his tool shed one Saturday morning in early summer and asked, "You are not French, are you?

"No, I'm from Sicily."

"But are you happy here?" replied Michel.

"Yes, of course, but I would be happy anywhere there is good soil, sunshine, and a few seeds to plant. Those are the things I love. And, of course, I grow things in my garden for people I love. Without sharing things, well you might as well be a monk, I suppose, praying all the time and contemplating God. I prefer to contemplate vegetables; not just any vegetables mind you, but my perfect vegetables. You should see the joy on Sister Esme's face when I bring her the first spring cuttings of my asparagus—with all her books and her art; they're no match for my asparagus! It is perhaps not always easy to find out what you love, but we must all make the effort. And, uh, where are you from, my boy?"

"I'm not sure exactly, somewhere near here, but maybe some other place."

"Oh, I see. But perhaps you can be happy here as well," said Tommasso while methodically cleaning his scythe.

Within a few days Michel volunteered after school to do odd jobs for Tommasso in the garden. He weeded the rows of lettuce and green beans and gathered the cuttings from the large vegetable plot and placed them on the compost pile. He shoveled out the straw in the stalls for the workhorses that plowed the fields and pulled the carriages. At first, Tommasso was somewhat apprehensive about the potential reaction of the nuns to the boy's helping him. At sixty-three, slightly stooped and more deliberate in his gait, there was little left of the physical prowess of young lancer who at nineteen had left Palermo for Marseilles and volunteered for the Franco-Prussian War. No, Tommasso did not wish to compromise his comfortable position at the orphanage and the garden he loved, but he did feel an affinity for the boy. He spoke directly to Sister Catherine who had responsibility for the gardens. He explained with exaggerated gestures that while he did not really need any extra help, Michel seemed to enjoy the fresh air. He had no objection to Michel doing odd jobs for him. Sister Catherine agreed to let him work in the garden with Tommasso as long as Michel kept up with his studies and was cleaned up for the evening meal at 7:00.

Initially there were times when communication between the two of them proved somewhat difficult. Michel on occasion misunderstood Tommasso's slurred accent, which was peppered with army slang. After several months went by and their friendship grew, Tommasso began to tell Michel his favorite stories, and it was through these tales that Michel grew to know and understand a great deal about how Tommasso saw the world. At the end of the day's work when the last tool was cleaned and then placed on it's hook in the shed and the travertine sky began to fade, Tommasso would lean against the wheel of the carriage and slowly, with great emphasis recount his favorite tale. The first tale was the legend of the construction of the great cathedral at Chartres. Only a few kilometers from the orphanage, its two great spires could be seen from the western gardens rising to the heavens and dominating the landscape. Michel at first thought the spires must be from a castle of a great king.

Pointing to the lofty, delicate spires, Michel asked, "Is that where the king and queen live?"

"No, Michel," replied Tommasso, "this place was not for kings and queens, but a place built by common people to worship God. As Sister Esme always says, those spires are the outstretched fingers of mankind trying to caress the face of God. There are many beautiful cathedrals in France and in Italy, to be sure. What makes Chartres different than all others is not just its beauty, but the spirit of joy the people experienced in building it. That spirit lives on and enriches us to this day. You see, Michel, for thousands of people, selecting each individual stone for the cathedral was an act of great worship. From all over France and Christendom, men and women, rich and poor, came together out of their love for God to take part in the building of the cathedral. And some day, when you are a bit older, I will take you there to see it. You will see the famous stained glass and other sights like nowhere else in this world. But you must first know the story of the building of the cathedral, for it is a wondrous tale."

And so Tommasso explained that the original church was built at Chartres to commemorate one of the most sacred medieval relics of all Christendom, the tunic of the Blessed Virgin. He went to tell all about the crusades and how the nobles and knights fought the infidels who had captured the Holy Lands. It was the crusaders who discovered the tunic that had been hidden since Mary's ascension to heaven. The crusading knights then brought it to Constantinople for safe-keeping and then Charlemagne himself transported it back to his court in Europe. His grandson was charged with the task of finding a place to build a church to sanctify the relic and he selected Chartres from all the possible towns in Europe. The modest church that was erected for the tunic attracted many pilgrims and brought much good fortune to the town.

Tragically, one night during the Middle Ages the church burned to the ground. Everyone was distraught that the tunic and its powerful aura were lost to humankind forever. One of the parish priests, however, was divinely inspired to dig one corner of the ruins, shouting with fevered pitch, "Help me dig, everyone, help me everyone, I know it is here!" Soon all the townsfolk were assisting him in the excavation, carrying away the charred beams and fragmented windows in any carts they could find. In a tiny crypt buried deep beneath the foundation of the collapsed church, they miraculously recovered the tunic unharmed.

The bishop and the villagers were so overcome with joy at the miracle that they immediately began the construction of one of the finest Gothic cathedrals in all the land to preserve the relic. The intense feeling of religious joy that swept over the people bound them all together in the great cause. Rich and poor, nobles and serfs, priests and peasants—all took part in the building. They left their villages and cottages and castles to live and work together for the massive effort.

They each pushed their own small cart for miles through rain and cold with the heavy stones from distant quarries. Skilled craftsman, stonemasons, carpenters, and glaziers came from all over Europe to help in the grand endeavor with no thought of payment or recognition. Although it took decades, the great cathedral was finished sooner than anyone could possibly have imagined and stands today over many centuries as the monument to that joyous feeling so long ago. To this day, no one knows the name of the architect or the engineers that designed and built the cathedral. No one wanted to take credit for this building inspired by God.

No matter how often he heard the tale of the great cathedral and began to recognize Tommasso's numerous slight variations, that intense feeling of community and devotion that fell over the land always captivated Michel. If time allowed before the evening meal, Tommasso would tell a second story. It was this second story, however, that had a profound impact on Michel. It was the story of Tommasso's trip with his father as a small boy growing up in Sicily and to see a great painting by Caravaggio.

Tommasso's mother died of fever in Palermo when he was barely five. For weeks after her death, his father could not eat or care for his son. The parish priest begged him to take his son on a pilgrimage to Syracuse to pray to Saint Lucy for consolation. Ultimately he agreed and they undertook the three-day overland journey by mule-drawn cart and reached the small chapel for the patron saint of the city. It was not, however, the response to my father's prayers for Saint Lucy that brought him consolation. Rather, it was an encounter with a painting that hung directly above the chapel altar that brought him peace.

Tommasso described the painting, Caravaggio's "The Burial of Saint Lucy," as an enormous masterpiece covering an entire wall. The upper two-thirds of the painting consisted almost entirely of somber shadows. Descending from this darkness, Saint Lucy rested on the ground, with a soft amber light on her face illuminating an unmistakable serenity. In the foreground, simple peasants overcome with grief furiously dug into the ground to bury the body of the saint. Tommasso and his father could easily recognize the faces in the painting as people one could meet in any market in Sicily. Tommasso's father stared at the painting for a long time and then slowly fell to his knees and wept.

A Franciscan friar who had been standing behind him slowly came forward and put his hand on my father's shoulder as he sobbed. My father said to him, "Tell me, Friar, why does this painting affect me so?"

The friar asked him to stand up and follow him, and they walked together toward the nave of the church were there was a fine piece of sculpture. He said to my father, "Look at this pietà. It is sculpted from the most beautiful marble by the hand of one of Italy's finest artists. Its power comes from the mirror it holds up to God. Caravaggio's power, my son, comes from the mirror he holds up to the soul of man. Caravaggio was a tortured man, they say—a fallen Templar Knight. Some even say he was a murderer. It is no matter; we are all sinners in the sight of God. But his power, as you felt it when you saw his painting, reflects God's forgiveness for our sins that is achieved in the peace after death."

And so my father and I left the church. He then embraced me saying, "Now we can make the journey back. I have received a sign from this painting."

As a boy Tommasso did not understand the meaning of the painting or his father's reaction to it. Later, as a young man about to leave his country and travel to France to volunteer into the army, he visited Syracuse and witnessed the painting one more time. Only then did he understand the acceptance of death his father had found in the interplay of shadow and light. Tommasso said to Michel that the soul of man is knowable only to God, but sometimes a hint of it is revealed in a great work of art. This phrase would resonate in Michel's mind.

There were days, however, when Michel still misunderstood Tommasso's instructions in the fields. Confronted by a perplexing request one afternoon, Michel withdrew to Tommasso's shed. He emerged minutes later with an extraordinarily precise sketch of their workhorse drawn with pencil on the back of a bill for fertilizer.

Tommasso stopped raking and leaned against a fencepost amazed by the many intricate details of the mane and head of the horse. He soon exclaimed, "Yes, my boy, it's the stalls that I want you to clean next."

From that day onward when the afternoon work was done Tommasso encouraged Michel to make more pencil drawings. Soon sketches of hollyhocks, corn stalks, and vines growing along the fieldstone hedgerow were hung on the wooden door of the shed. At first, Tommasso supplied the paper from old inventory slips, but soon ran out and had to request used paper from the village printer on market days when he sold his excess vegetables from the garden.

The enthusiasm for Michel's newfound artistic expression, however, was not shared by the orphanage hierarchy. When Sister Monique, the head sister, entered the shed one morning to look for Tommasso, she was startled first and then infuriated by the large number of pencil and charcoal sketches that seemed to cover every inch of wall space. At the bottom of each one of the sketches lying on the cluttered desk was written in a juvenile cursive "for Tommasso."

She sat impatiently on a wooden stool with her crossed legs sawing furiously back and forth waiting for Tommasso to return. As he entered, she burst out at him, "What is the meaning of this? These pictures, these…these drawings. Sister Catherine told me Michel was learning the trade of a gardener while helping you to do chores. I do not approve of this wasteful time spent on drawing."

Tommasso was completely taken off guard at these pointed remarks and offered defensively, "But please, let me explain, these sketches were done only after work and are harmless and…"

She did not let him finish and remarked briskly, "And so you shall explain. I will expect you in my office this evening immediately after evening prayers."

After she left, Tommasso sat down and thought to himself about Michel's drawing. He looked at the many sketches on the shed walls and was struck by the subjects that came to life with his pencil. He thought to himself, "I will tell that old witch the truth. Yes, Michel sketches when the chores are done. It is his one joy, his passion. If Sister Monique is unwilling to accept that and it costs me my job, then so be it."

That evening at nine o'clock, Tommasso, freshly shaven and dressed in his only suit of clothes, entered the back entrance to the gray fieldstone office building and began to walk slowly down its long corridor. Tommasso came here generally only a few times a year, once at Christmas time to receive his meager bonus and then in early April to have Sister Monique grudgingly approve his inventory request for seeds and fertilizer for the springtime planting. The scant lighting from the twenty-foot ceilings cast long shadows from the diminutive man walking down the broad hallway. The daily ritual overseen by Sister Monique of scrubbing of the marble floors with dilute carbolic acid created a smell that was repugnant to Tommasso. The intense fragrance of a small bouquet of lavender and peonies he carried in his hand was as much a defensive distraction for him as a peace offering to Sister Monique. Passing him furtively in the corridor were several small groups of nuns coming from the chapel seeming to avoid him with only minimal murmuring of recognition as if they feared association with his censure.

The door to the office complex was deliberately left open, suggesting that his rebuke would be a matter and for all to hear. Sister Monique sat behind an imposing cherry desk surrounded by shelves containing her collection of the writings of early church fathers. Her scholarship in this area was beginning to receive modest attention from the bishop. She held out the hope that his recognition might enable her to transfer to a much more important post in Paris or Rouen.

Despite the offering of Tommasso's bouquet, Sister Monique immediately went on the offensive. She rose from her chair and the small table lamp eerily illuminated her face, "Let me speak plainly and forthrightly, Tommasso. I will not have you exceed your authority and give false expectations to this Arab boy. It is unfair to him to mislead him into thinking that he can somehow become an artist. Art has its role I suppose in the church and elsewhere, but if this boy is to get on in life he must learn a trade. We are not an academy for misguided 'Titians.' Do you understand what I'm saying?"

"I do, Sister, but I would only say that I have seen in the boy's eyes the joy and delight this skill brings to him. You see, he is not like the other boys. And he wishes to have something, something of his own. The boys at the orphanage all wear the same uniforms, study the same books, and take the same meals at the same time. This love for drawing is the one thing that he has of his own. It is his passion."

"You will not contradict me on this matter, and if you are suggesting..."

At that point, a loud voice came from the corridor as Sister Esme entered the office, "Well, as long as we are having a public discussion about this matter, you might indulge the senior sister and permit me to offer some advice." Sister Esme strode into the office with a confidence and air in confronting Sister Monique that Tommasso found perplexing, but refreshing. Sister Esme was short with black robes overflowing her ample girth. For many years she had been in charge of cataloguing the large collection of medieval texts in the chapel's scriptorium. It was her discovery of several forgotten illuminated manuscripts concerning the early church fathers that had, in fact, propelled Sister Monique's research. It was this intellectual dependency more than her seniority that gave her a unique leverage to address Sister Monique directly.

Sister Esme said, "Before I begin, remind me, Sister Monique, to share with you a new reference I have just discovered on Saint Aquinas. It is a most remarkable find and one that I hope you will find quite interesting. But as to the matter of the boy's interest in art and drawing, I can only echo your concern that this not become a distraction from his studies or his other Christian responsibilities here at the orphanage. Assured of that, I see no harm in the boy pursuing this most trivial of passions. We all need to pursue our passions, don't we, Sister Monique? Along with our passion for Christ, of course. I too share a love for art along with the boy, but sadly without the capacity to create it. Yes, we must all approach life with our God-given passions. Now run along Tommasso and find a vase for those flowers. I shall be delighted to oversee the boy's progress from time to time and relieve the Sister of any lingering concern for its appropriateness. By the way, Sister, the boy is half-French."

That was officially the end of the matter. Over the next few weeks, Sister Esme praised and encouraged Michel's drawing. She found an old sketchbook left in a trunk by one of the nuns who had resigned her vows. She displayed her favorite works by Michel in the younger children's classroom. For his ninth birthday Tommasso was allowed to purchase a watercolor set with brushes for Michel from the village. This was in lieu of the traditional pair of new socks or pullover that the parish provided. Every free moment, it seemed, Michel would experiment mixing different shades of vivid colors and soon had a small portfolio to show Tommasso.

Intuitively, Sister Esme understood that Michel was emotionally different from the other children. His mixed racial features, in addition, would make life after the orphanage challenging. Michel had few friends among the other children. She realized that his artistic talents would be, if nothing else, an important refuge in a life that otherwise held few advantages.

One April, Tommasso entered one of Michel's landscape watercolors in a competition at the village art fair. His winning painting was displayed for the school in a small wooden frame on the courtyard wall outside the library. During a chance encounter on the way back from sketching, Michel saw from a distance Camille Richard staring at his painting. Since their dramatic confrontation two years previously, there had been little interaction between them. He stopped and curiously observed that she twice went up to look closely at the name printed next to the small ribbon. For Michel the feelings of isolation and rejection associated with Camille's outbursts had faded. His friendship with Tommasso and his growing interest in painting had filled that void. Gone too were the bushy childish bangs covering Camille's eyes. Her reddish brown hair was elegantly pulled back from her face befitting her status as a soloist in the choir.

Michel stopped in the courtyard and unconsciously took out a charcoal pencil and rapidly drew the outline of her features in profile. When Camille turned around and looked at Michel, he pretended to be fumbling through his notebook. As she passed him, she looked straight ahead with only a faint mumbling of "Congratulations" as she entered the library.

The orphanage's spartan dormitory was built in an L-shaped configuration representing half of a quadrangle that was never completed. Over three hundred or so children aged four to sixteen were housed in a three-story brick building that chronically suffered from an inadequate central heating. Gusting winds off the plains of Beauce penetrated the cracked and aging wooden window frames and were a torment throughout the winter months. In each wing of the dormitory, coal fireplaces were asymmetrically situated along the two long rows of the children's beds. The younger children were housed on the ground floor in two wings. The roughly sixty older boys slept on the second floor of the east wing and were segregated in two long rows according to age and alphabetical order of last names. The relatively small number of boys made it possible in winter to huddle the beds around the four fireplaces and away from the worst-offending widow panes. This simple solution was not possible for the one hundred and fifty older girls overflowing both the second and third floors of the west wing. Sister Charisse, the girl's chaperone living on the third floor, concocted a competitive system of bed positioning rewarding the best students and most compliable girls with the most desirable bed locations. Not surprisingly, Camille's bed was not too close and not too far away from the best fireplace near the end of the third-floor room. Her window was one of the very few to have been replaced in the last decade. Michel's room on the second floor was in the same corner as Camille's.

Weeks of incessant rain in May made work in the gardens and outside excursions impossible, so Michel began painting scenes from library books or doing portraits of willing roommates. At the end of the second week, Tommasso was suddenly called away to the funeral in Lille of his old commanding officer. Michel had never seen Tommasso so overcome with emotion and realized how important his few remaining friends from the army were to him. During this same period, Sister Esme was also in Paris overseeing the restoration of a medieval manuscript. For the first time he could remember, Michel had no one to show his paintings to. It was as if much of the joy had been taken out of it. It wasn't simply a matter of praise that he missed, for on occasion Tommasso would hint that he could perhaps do better. No, he was learning that a great part of the pleasure of creating the painting was sharing it with others.

Staring out the corner window of his room one gray afternoon, Michel saw Camille on the floor above cleaning and rearranging some books that she had placed on the windowsill. Michel timidly waved at her and caught her attention, but she immediately stopped and walked away from the window. Undaunted, Michel remembered his partially completed charcoal sketch of Camille and finished it from memory. He placed it in the window late that afternoon where Camille could see it. At different times that afternoon until the light faded, he caught glimpses of her staring at the picture. He tried to think of things that would interest her and so several days later he painted a picture of choir rehearsal in the chapel and placed that in his window as well. Again he could see that Camille discreetly took pains to examine the painting. Yet she still mistrusted him and refused to say anything more than a perfunctory greeting as she rushed by the school corridor.

CHAPTER 10

▼

"Is it wrong to cherish things of art if they praise God? Is it blasphemy to adore such things of beauty and mystery? Of angels and saints in the golden margins of a book reflecting God's glory? Is it wrong to keep this book hidden, like a small jewel forgotten to all, known only to me? I alone know its power to inspire, more than any priest's words of faith can inspire. Yes, it is wrong, I suppose, to keep it to myself. But I accept that just the same. What would I have without it?"

—Sister Esme

On the eastern grounds of the orphanage adjacent to the nondescript brick façade of the dormitories was the diminutive, ancient stone chapel with its vaulted ceiling and graceful arches. A musty scriptorium with three oak benches and tall metal-caged shelves extended from the east wing of the chapel. Decades ago Sister Monique had assigned Sister Esme the task of inventorying all of the manuscripts, which dated back to the late thirteenth century. From time to time church scholars would visit from Paris or Rouen to examine the old leather and velum texts many with inlaid semiprecious jewels. They were hoping to find architectural clues about the mysterious construction of the great cathedral at Chartres, for which no records could be found. The architect had been anonymous, preferring posterity to be less concerned with the technical feat of its human construction and more responsive to its aesthetic power.

At seventy-two, Sister Esme could not remember a time when she had not felt her life's rhythms regimented by the bells of matins and evening prayers. Her dying father's wish was for her to take the vows, or so her stepmother had claimed. But, no matter, a life in the church was an acceptable life perhaps, no worse than any other, and she had grown used to it. Sister Esme often thought of her younger sister Claire, who had visited her each Easter until she died two years ago. After the usual pleasantries, her sister would invariably confess her tale about her overbearing husband, his failing business, and her three demanding children.

No, she knew that there was no escaping the sorrows of this world. She understood, moreover, that without a life in the church, she would never have had the time or solitude to reflect upon the art she so dearly loved. To her, the art treasures of the church she had seen in Rome were man's greatest achievement. Creating true art as did da Vinci, Giotto, and Raphael was a rare gift from God, and she felt deeply that art had a power to inspire beyond the artist. The artist may be too ensnared by the painting's immediate technical demands or temporal influence. Her unspoken personal religion was based on an understanding of how art pointed the way to God. She tried to convince herself that this truth was truly something worthy of one's life devotion. The scriptorium and the art treasures in its books had become her private, votive world. Here she could feel unashamed and embrace a world of devotion through artistic beauty.

Sister Esme, like many of the other sisters, had heard the rumors about Michel's artistic ability. One bright fall morning, seeing Michel talking with other boys at the back of the chapel after Sunday communion, she impulsively unlocked the wire frame door and asked him into the scriptorium. She lovingly and painstakingly withdrew from the top shelf a heavy leather-bound Bible she had discovered many years ago. Its plain, timeworn binding was clearly less impressive than some of the jeweled texts on the shelves. However, for her, it held a fascination like no other. Its intensely colored margins along the perfectly inscribed Latin narrative displayed arrow-pierced saints, divinely inspired apostles kneeling and caressing the sick, and angels with a strangely human sensibility. For her the greatest triumph of all was the depiction of Christ bearing his cross with an upturned face, radiant in his forgiveness toward the derisive Roman soldiers.

Sister Esme, for the most part, kept this favorite text to herself. From time to time, however, she would unobtrusively turn its pages in the presence of the newer sisters or the occasional visiting scholar. Saying nothing, she was nonetheless intently interested in their spontaneous reaction to the artwork. Sister Esme often surreptitiously observed the response of others to the book's unexpectedly brilliant colors. Among the newly ordained sisters the fascination for the book seemed more like the delight of a child for a shiny Christmas toy. To the occasional visiting church scholar, the most common reaction was most often one of muted indifference or reflexive historical analysis.

There were minor, but discernible imperfections in the text visible only to a medieval scholar. Curiously, its style was not entirely representational of the late medieval art of the region. Its subtle humanism departed from the stereotypical Byzantine sensibility preferred by most experts. Sister Esme loved it precisely for its unique individualistic imagery of Jesus and the saints. Its imperfections only seemed to enhance its value to her knowing that the scholars had missed an essential truth she alone had found. She was enormously grateful that her Bible was not selected to be sent away for cleaning or restoration and therefore, never to return from the College de France or the Sorbonne.

Over the years, however, she gradually became aware how her own reaction to the book could subtly change with her frame of mind. It vacillated in a small, but finite way depending on the strength of her faith. In those infrequent, but exhilarating moments when she seemed to sense the immediacy of God's love, she experienced a profound connection to the anonymous medieval monks who depicted a humanistic Christ and the saints in the book's margins. They did not seem to her to be abstract icons, but real individuals struggling to be worthy of God's grace in this world and not the next. As she gazed at the faces of the tortured saints, she felt as if the monks were speaking lovingly to her. The fact that she could hear these voices validated in some small way her choice to leave behind a predictable life of family, children, and suitors for a different kind of love. She became aligned with the ancient artist monks on a profound emotional level. The art seemed to transcend the work of a single individual created in her an aura of devotional energy.

During less exultant times when she was beset with a longing for another kind of life or experiencing doubt about her faith, Sister Esme took refuge in these golden pictures. She took comfort in the forbidden knowledge that she alone had the unique ability to respond to their hidden truth.

Sister Esme watched as Michel now gazed at the ancient text and its mysterious images. He was silent and motionless for a long time. He then moved his hand, as if by some gravitational pull, slowly and deliberately along the book's golden margin a few inches above the page. He looked directly at sister Esme and said softly, "Thank you, Sister Esme, it's so beautiful."

And so Michel began painting with watercolors with her each Sunday afternoon after mass in the scriptorium. Under the seemingly detached, but approving eye of Sister Esme, he chose initially to copy scenes from the biblical text in brilliant hues of gold and blue. Within a few months, however, he stopped trying to merely copy the images in her favorite text and began to impart his own sense of humanity to the saints, apostles, and biblical characters. He painted ordinary people with recognizable emotions.

Sister Esme rarely commented beyond a few simple words of encouragement: "What an artist you've become. And you can see how much, Michel, the church values its artists. The saints and apostles come alive with your brush. Of course, even painting a bowl of fruit or a scene from the countryside takes a measure of skill, but, to capture the truth of human emotions with your brush, Michel, now that is real art."

From time to time, Michel would paint other subjects, such as the chapel's vaulted ceiling, its stained glass windows, and carved wooden pulpit. However, he would inevitably return to the images of the saints. Sister Esme gradually began to see in his work not just the technical skill of a prodigy, but someone who saw a religious world from a unique emotional vantage point. She recognized his ability to project a persona into the saints well beyond the uniformity and homogeneity depicted in the ancient texts. Their human expressions in his works created subtle moods encompassing a range of human emotions from undeniable bliss to equally recognizable pain and anxiety. She looked forward each week to their private time they spent together, but Sister Esme knew that to be a true artist Michel would have to experience the world and paint from a wellspring of his own source.

Two weeks after his twelfth birthday, Tommasso called Michel into the shed, which now was overflowing with artwork from every wall. "On June 21st, Michel, I will take you to see the great cathedral. I've already spoken with Sister Monique. You will ride with me in the cart at dawn on market day into Chartres."

On June 20th, Michel learned of their trip to the cathedral the next morning and he lay awake all night trying to imagine what he might feel in the presence of such a sacred place. At four o'clock in the morning, he crept out of the dormitory in the dark with his paints and brushes in a small wooden box and his easel under his arm. He met Tommasso at the barn already sitting in the horse-drawn wagon. As they traversed the paved streets in the faint moonlight and neared the massive carved doors of the east portal of Chartres, they saw a man carrying a small candle. He met them warmly and offered hot tea. After a few excited greetings and sips of tea, he ushered them into a side door and along a narrow marble passageway. After walking a few dozen paces, the man motioned for them to sit on a small stone bench carved in the wall. Spreading a small woolen blanket he said, "Please, sit. We must wait here until the first rays of dawn illuminate the great windows. Then, you will see it. You will see!"

Michel looked up and in the dim candlelight could barely discern the vast vaulted ceiling and stained glass windows of the cathedral's eastern wall. He leaned his head on Tommasso's shoulder for a moment and then promptly fell asleep. When Tommasso gently rubbed his arm and told him to wake, he heard the man talking in hushed, but animated tones. And then the first shafts of light appeared through the vibrantly colored stained glass windows of the great eastern wall.

Tommasso could not keep silent and whispered, "Oh, each year it is more beautiful than I remember! See there, over there, where the streams of light cross. There it is!"

What frightened and then amazed Michel was the scale and seemingly limitlessness dimensions of cathedral's inner space. Then he followed Tommasso's hand to see the golden shafts of light emerging from the brilliant garnet, blue, and emerald stained glass windows that intersected on the mosaic floor of the nave in the unmistakable pattern of a cross.

Then Tommasso said, "The light is incredible. I have never seen the shafts glow like that. The light surrounds us every day of our lives. It surrounds us all the time and yet we do not perceive it or know it is there. Like God's love, like God's love."

They were all silent for a moment and then Michel said, "But it's the windows. They are so beautiful. It's the windows made by man that allow us to see the light made by God."

As the light slowly diffused around them, Michel held his easel and paints under his arm. Tommasso then said, "You must paint quickly. People will be coming for mass and we must not let the priest see you."

Michel set sown his easel and opened his small wooden box of paints that contained several completed watercolors of the chapel in Courville. He spread them out on the stone bench and began to paint the cathedral's streaming shafts of light. Tommasso watched as Michel quickly sketched the composition with charcoal on one sheet of paper. Once satisfied with the sketch, Michel then began to quickly mix the watercolors and paint. He soon realized that the intense hues of the windows could not be adequately captured by his pale watercolors, but Michel held this thought aside and did his best to capture the feeling of the scene. Within a few minutes, the bells began and several older women murmured as they entered the cathedral to light candles and pray.

As Michel worked intently, Tommasso sensed the presence of someone watching them in the shadows of the passageway. Just as Michel was finishing and gathering up his paintings, a tall thin man in a white linen suit approached them. As he held a large brimmed hat to his right shoulder a narrow shadow extended from his reddish goatee to the royal blue silk handkerchief in his jacket.

"You'll excuse me," he said. "I could not help but notice the boy painting. No doubt he is quite a prodigy. If I might, I wonder if you would permit me to purchase one of these fine paintings. Shall we say, fifty francs?"

Fifty francs was more than a month's salary, yet Tommasso replied unhesitatingly, "The paintings are not for sale."

"Very, well. I can certainly understand. Please permit me an observation then. As you are likely to discover, my boy, watercolors, although possessing a certain charm, cannot do justice to a scene of this intensity. Only oils can accomplish that. It is quite a transition to oil painting, you know, but it is inevitable for one with such talent. But the art of painting requires many years of tutelage and study. All the great painters have learned from a master."

The man then took out a card and a pen from a leather wallet in his suit jacket. Writing in brusque stroke, he then spoke directly to Tommasso, "Fortunately, an exceptionally able artist who is also a business associate of mine might be willing to take on the task of training such a talent. Here is his address on rue Jacob and the address of our gallery in Paris. Perhaps one day our paths will cross. It is an excellent idea to paint the lights, but perhaps too demanding a subject for such a young boy."

CHAPTER 11

▼

By the time they were both fourteen, Michel and Camille had developed very different attitudes toward their artistic endeavors and how they thought about their art in relation to their identity. For Michel, painting was a natural extension of himself and how he thought and saw the world around him, but he had little concept of himself as an "artist." His daily painting and sketching were part of his most anticipated pleasures, equal to working with Tommasso and his friendship with Sister Esme. He certainly relished the notoriety he received by winning several small prizes at the local art fairs, but he had not yet thought of pursing art as his life's work. Camille's attitude toward her singing, however, was strikingly different. A year before at the bishop's annual music festival, Camille had heard opera sung for the first time. A duet from Verdi was a transformational experience. She heard secular music for the first time and was amazed by its beauty, power, and drama. Moreover, she saw in the soprano a role that was intended and designed for women without having to justify her involvement in music. Despite the many obstacles that lay ahead, Camille knew that this was the career path that she would follow. Her most immediate need was a voice teacher and mentor to help her begin the journey.

Learning of Camille's grand design to become an opera singer, Sister Esme offered enthusiasm tempered with a tinge of realism. "It is wonderful that you have chosen to follow your passion for singing, Camille. You will have to study a bit of German and Italian. We, of course, have Tommasso and Sister Gertrude to help with that. Then there is the matter of finding you a voice instructor. You will need to develop a repertoire and to train your voice professionally in order to be accepted as an apprentice in one of the great opera companies in Paris. I will ask Monsieur Truffant, who is choirmaster at Chartres, if there is someone suitable in the area. But there is one final complication, the matter of paying for the lessons. Here we may need outside help to raise a bit of money. I know that things between you and Michel have not always been, well, cordial, but it's now time to bury the hatchet. I believe that we may need Michel's artistic assistance. I should think that painted postcards of the great cathedral would sell quite handsomely in the market place. Don't you think so? I'm sure if I ask him, Michel will agree. Sister Monique might not approve, of course, but I'm not certain we shall tell her."

Michel did agree, but Monsieur Truffant, as it turned out, was somewhat offended by Sister Esme's delicate inquiry into the realm of secular music. However, an elderly man in the choir came up to Sister Esme, after overhearing the conversation with a hushed referral. "It's Madame Petrovski you want. Lives just outside Thivars, I think. I heard her several years ago at the recital for the spring festival. There's none like her in these parts. A bit odd she married that Polish fellow, but when she's of a mind to she can still hit the high notes all right."

That Sunday afternoon Sister Esme and Camille rode by carriage to the neighboring village of Thivars. Madame Petrovski was well known to the local farmers, who pointed out the imposing mansion in the distance just west of town. As they slowly approached the main house from the long driveway of loose gravel, the parallel rows of once-sculpted yew trees gave the feeling of a faded elegance of a different time. It was also the impression of the petty bourgeoisie happily ensconced in the countryside and relieved to be beyond the scrutiny of their more stylistically conscious urban counterparts. The cream-colored exterior of the house with its pale blue shutters reflected cheerfulness more reminiscent of a Provençal farmhouse than anything from the plains of Beauce.

The elderly maid who greeted them at the door seemed genuinely glad to have company on this overcast afternoon. She led them down a dimly lit corridor of worn oriental rugs and gas lamps draped with gold and scarlet fringe into a sunlit music room of oversized palms, and floor-to-ceiling windows in their wrought iron frames. From behind a grand piano, a small woman emerged wearing a blue paisley shawl with her graying hair pulled back and covered with a blue silk scarf.

"To whom do we owe this delightful visit?" she said.

"How do you do, Madame, I am Sister Esme and this is Camille. Camille Richard. We are from the orphanage in Courville and have come to enquire about singing lessons."

"What a lovely child. And you must be eleven...twelve years old?"

"Twelve, Madame." Camille spoke up.

"Well, not a moment too soon. We'll have some tea, Anna. Sister Esme, please be seated on the sofa. You, child, please sit next to me here by the piano. Now just follow along and sing as I play this scale."

Camille sang with such strength and clarity that Madame Petrovski cut short the impromptu audition by simply remarking, "Splendid, my child. Now as you are from the orphanage, I will reduce my customary fee and you will pay me only five francs per session when it is convenient. I shall expect you each Sunday at one o'clock. Camille, you must promise me that you will not waste this opportunity and you will practice faithfully and make us all very proud of you."

"Oh, I shall Madame, I truly shall."

And so each Sunday after mass, Camille and Michel would bicycle together to Madame Petrovski's house for her lessons. Then Michel would continue on to Chartres with his leather satchel on his back containing the half-dozen painted postcards he would sell in the square outside the cathedral. At four o'clock after most of the tourists had gone back to the train station, Michel would make the return trip to Thivars and wait outside on the lawn for Camille to finish. For the first several weeks that spring, Camille was quite reserved on their trips, overcome with both the excitement of her new venture and yet afraid that without the help of Michel it would not be possible. She half-expected his altruism in financing the lessons to fade as there seemed very little for him to gain in the bargain other than the effort to churn out and then sell dozens of postcards. Camille had grown up to be innately suspicious of men, whether as a result of her abusive father or Monsieur Elluard's hostility. So she reserved judgment about Michel as part of her distrustful inclination.

That suspicion ended one Saturday when Michel was taken sick and admitted to the infirmary with a fever. Camille went to visit him before mass on Sunday and found him asleep, but with an easel and watercolors next to his bed containing a half-finished postcard. From that moment forward, she began to trust Michel and when he recovered from his illness she looked forward to their trips and talked continuously about anything and everything about life at the orphanage and her future dreams.

One hot day in August as Michel sat under a wisteria arbor in Madame Petrovski's yard, Camille said goodbye at the doorstep. Madame Petrovski saw Michel lying on the grass and invited him in for iced tea.

"And who is your nice young escort, my dear?"

"His name is Michel, Madame. Michel Hassan. He is from the orphanage."

"Splendid. Please ask him to join us for a cold drink." As they were served iced tea on the patio shaded by beech trees, Madame Petrovski continued, "Hassan, you said. Many years ago I recall a man of that name. Let me try to remember. Yes, I think he may have been my friend Julia's son-in-law. Yes, Julia, who lived not three miles from here before she died."

Michel spoke excitedly, "I believe that you might be referring to my grandmother Julia. I'm told she lived somewhere near Thivars."

Madame Petrovski sat up in her chair with a start, and called out to her servant, "Anna, please bring me Aimee's photo album from her wedding reception. It's in the living room near the ottoman. I do believe I may have a surprise for you, Michel."

The servant soon appeared with an oversized photo album and placed it on the table. After leafing through it for several minutes, Madame Petrovski exclaimed, "Yes, here is the photograph I was searching for. Julia came to my daughter's wedding reception and her daughter was one of Aimee's good friends. She brought along her new husband. Here. And you can see, Michel, your father was quite the dashing officer in his uniform."

Michel immediately got up from his chair and peered intently at the picture. Madame Petrovski knew immediately by his reaction that there was a good chance that Michel had never seen a picture of his father before. After a few moments she remarked, "It would please me very much if you would take this picture, Michel. Your grandmother, Julia, was such a dear friend and, well, it is always good to have an extra family picture, isn't it Michel?"

"Yes, I suppose it is," he replied without taking his gaze off the photo.

Over the next few weeks, Camille began unconsciously to open up and to trust Michel unlike anyone else before. At times she was taken aback by her own loquaciousness and how much she wished to tell him about her aspirations and plans. She would lie in bed at night and think to herself that somehow it was all meant to happen. Her voice lessons financed by Michel's painting and the chance sharing of Madame Petrovski's photograph—it all must be part of something larger and more important rather than sheer coincidence.

Camille had known her father all too well and spent much of her time at the orphanage trying to free herself from his oppressive memory. Michel had never known his father and possibly never would have, but for a random meeting of an acquaintance. His imagination roamed widely about what his father did and felt. One thing was for certain; he was indeed a French army officer. Tommasso confirmed this fact as soon he was shown the picture.

"He was a captain in the French army alright, Michel. I'd recognize those epaulets anywhere. Looks like the Algerian insignia on the shoulder to me, but it's hard to make out. Knowing what I know of the French army, Michel, your father must have been…well, let's just say a leader anyone could recognize," said Tommasso gently.

CHAPTER 12

▼

When Michel turned fifteen, Tommasso obtained permission from the nuns to bring him into the village for a birthday dinner. After a fine meal and some spirited conversation about their times together, Tommasso grew more serious on the carriage ride back and leaned over to Michel and said, "I suspect you'll be leaving sooner than the sisters think. You'll not wait to be transferred to some factory in Paris when you turn sixteen. You're as big as a grown man already. Well, I won't wait much longer either. This is a fine place, but my home is in Sicily. My sister is not well. I have never seen her children, you know. There are so many stories there I want to relearn. Now that you are a man, my work at the orphanage is finished. So, I have something for you."

Handing over a small cloth purse, he said, "You'll forgive me, but I sold several sketches to the gallery owner we met years ago at the cathedral. A respectable sum, enough for a start. And here is the address of my old commanding officer outside of Marseilles. He has a farm there and is always looking for hands. The army was my other family you see. I leave for Palermo tomorrow to finally see my sister. I know you will be a great painter, Michel. But you cannot rush it. You must first experience life and embrace it in all its joys and all its sorrows. I did that by joining the army. That's an introduction to life's sorrows, all right. But whatever you chose, chose life. Good-bye, my boy."

The following morning, with the vegetable fields plowed and planted, Tommasso hugged Michel and left in a carriage for the train station. Michel for the first time in years felt inconsolably alone. He knew that in several months, once he turned sixteen, he would leave, too, but without Tommasso he could not bear to walk by the gardens or even think of painting. He could not sleep and his thoughts wondered randomly. He thought of Camille and the fact that they had grown close together over the years. They talked after school the day after Tommasso left. Camille had to stay and play by the rules. She would live with Madame Petrovski after turning sixteen but would need two more years of studying German and Italian and additional voice lessons to have any chance of being taken on by one of the large opera companies in Paris. Michel gave her half the money from Tommasso over her strenuous objections. Two weeks later Michel planned his departure for Paris. He gathered several of his favorite watercolors and carefully placed them in an old briefcase.

Early on the morning of his departure, he went into the scriptorium for the last time. Sister Esme was in her usual chair surrounded by her usual pile of manuscripts. She looked up and instinctively knew he would be leaving and said without leaving her seat, "I shall tell them you are likely headed for Marseilles. That should give you the head start you need. And be sure to hide your bicycle well at the train station in Chartres. We don't want to leave any immediate evidence, now do we? I shall expect a letter at Christmas time with a full progress report on your painting. I will see to Camille and she will be fine with Madame Petrovski, I'm sure. Michel, I have no words of wisdom other than I know if you follow your heart you will be doing the right thing. And, as for Camille, life has many complexities. God is a help to some in difficulty, but love seems to me to help even more. Now be off with you before somebody sees you."

By nightfall Michel was wandering the narrow alleys near Notre Dame searching for a small portal to the larger world.

CHAPTER 13

▼

A disheveled man cradled in the doorway pointed halfheartedly down the darkened alley. Few of the hallway lamps were lit as Michel climbed the five flights of stairs at 19 rue Jacob. He cautiously clung to the leather case under his arm containing his most prized possessions. The dim light and thin layer of soot could not conceal the once-elegant carvings of the oak banister. Michel's thoughts, however, were entirely fixed on the man he soon would meet. He found that the large mahogany door to the studio was unlocked. Pungent and unfamiliar smells were mildly disorienting as he entered the cavernous room that occupied the top floor. Surrounded by rows of canvases covered completely with burlap was a small man in a chair reading by an oil lamp.

"Are you the one they call Carvalho?" Michel asked.

"Yes, who sent you?"

"A tall man I met several years ago at Chartres cathedral. He was wearing a white suit and had a reddish beard. He said you could teach me to paint."

"A reddish beard. Ah, yes, Victor, our famous friend. I see. Well, I'm sorry to disappoint you, but I'm afraid Nilhenkov was wrong. I cannot teach you to paint. No more than I can teach you to see or to breathe. If you want to learn a useful trade, learn how to draw. There are a dozen salons in Paris that can do that."

Michel did not answer. He slowly looked around at the few remaining paintings left uncovered and visible in the dim light. The sparse brush strokes triggered a thought in his mind, "You could paint at one time, but now you can't?"

The man said nothing. Michel continued, "Before I go, I want you to see these," Michel said as he extended the briefcase.

The man said nothing, but delicately inspected the ten watercolors of the saints Michel had chosen. He looked up at the tall, thin boy of sixteen with his brown skin and curly black hair.

"Tell me a painter you admire."

"Caravaggio." Michel replied without hesitation.

The man looked up and lunged forward in his chair visibly startled.

"Caravaggio, you say. Well, he's not much in favor these days, you know," the man said.

"Caravaggio," Michel said emphatically. "And one more artist, but I do not know his name."

"And who is that?"

"The one who conceived the stained glass windows at Chartres cathedral."

"Yes, the stained glass windows. I had almost forgotten them."

"But, I can only stay apprenticed to you for one year. Then I will join the army."

The man looked up, thought for a moment, and then said, "Confidence! I like that in a painter. Let's see if we can project that onto a canvas."

CHAPTER 14

▼

The man known as Carvalho was not only to become Michel's painting instructor for a year, but also a confidante and mentor. Some said that it was his equine facial features, his square jaw and oversized nose that was responsible for his nickname, which may have been a bastardized version of "horse" given to him by a Spanish mistress. In fact, his real name was Sergei Turnayev. Before fleeing czarist Russia, he was a feckless student from the minor nobility in fin de siècle Moscow. Sergei's true interest in art was not apparent at first and came about as an aberration of history and politics. To his diplomat father, Sergei's interminable studies were merely a ruse to conceal his real passions: gambling, pursuing the wives of senior military officers, and the social theory, if not the practice, of anarchist politics. On the other hand, Sergei's father fervently collected art throughout the capitals of Europe and Asia to such an extent that it strained both the family's financial resources and the patience of the czar's ministers. This led to his gradual loss of favor in higher diplomatic circles and it coincided with increasing scrutiny of Sergei's sporadic, but ardent political activities.

Sergei was not without his sentimental side, however, and refused to allow his father to dismiss his elderly nursemaid Anna. Sergei paid her meager wages from his own allowance and steadfastly refused to let his father rebuke Anna despite her evident idleness and incompetence as a housekeeper. Anna was by now a frail peasant with long braided white hair and watery blue eyes embedded in a labyrinth of deep brown wrinkles. As one of five servants in their larger Moscow apartment, Anna's only tasks were to wind the hallway clock, feed the cat, and dust the many scattered works of art in their imposing oak frames.

Anna's singular joy was her morning ritual of waking Sergei. At 10:00 AM she would slowly draw open the large brocade bedroom curtains and with elaborate deference bring him his breakfast tray and newspapers. But Sergei's part of the ritual was to first enquire about her dreams that night. "The dreams were very good, my boy, very good," she would invariably say.

But her response one morning in early June was quite different. "My dreams were not good, my boy. Not good." Then she said softly, but forthrightly, "We will leave for the summer house at once. I will tell the cook and the footman."

"Anna, how can we leave? It's right before my exams and you know the dacha will not be cleaned and ready until July."

Anna would hear none of his protestations and by late afternoon they began the five-hour journey by carriage. Unfortunately, after finding Sergei's vacant apartment, the czar's secret police were only hours behind.

Anna spoke little at the beginning of the trip and repetitively twisted her braids in a manner most disconcerting to Sergei. But after several hours of travel they were deep in the verdant countryside and both she and Sergei seemed in better spirits. It was exciting to leave at a moment's notice like a childhood adventure. When they arrived, however, Sergei was disappointed to hear Anna insist that he must sleep that night in the caretaker Alyosha's cottage in a back room attached to the barn. "Only when the dacha is cleaned properly can you go in it," said Anna.

Anna came to the caretaker's cottage at midnight to find Sergei and Alyosha playing cards by candlelight. She carried with her a diplomatic satchel Sergei recognized as his father's and placed it next to his feet. "Whatever happens, keep this with you. Now I will lock the door. Good night."

At four o'clock the next morning, hearing no response to their pounding on the front door of the dacha, the secret police fired two shots into its large iron padlock. By the time they finished searching the four dusty upstairs bedrooms and turned their attention to the cottage, Sergei was a mile away on Alyosha's best horse. A week later on the sleeper train from Vienna to Paris, Sergei discovered that the satchel held three signed sketches by Delacroix. Those bits of papers paid his entire expenses for two years in Paris. Sergei had learned the power of art and the power of dreams.

CHAPTER 15

▼

London, June, 1914

Dearest Michel,

Carvalho was kind enough to give me your address. It feels odd somehow for me to be the one writing to you about family and stability. My years of traipsing all over the capitals of Europe just to sing and wear those ridiculous costumes seems much less important to me now. You've been at the same army post in Toulon for three years and I've been constantly living out of a suitcase for nearly six. But I am the one longing for permanence now.

Michel, the only way I can tell you this is to be truthful and direct, one aspect of our relationship I truly cherish. I have met a man and fallen in love. An Englishman named Robert whom I met in Vienna. He followed me from Munich and Salzburg and was most persistent and charming. We will live in London part of the year during the opera season and then in the country. What I want most now is something you and I never had, a home and a family.

I know that when you asked me several years ago to marry you that I loved you. I always will, but at that time I could not bear to give up my dream of singing opera to be an army wife. I also know of your needs, your passion for painting, and your stable life you have found in the army. I have a different dream now, but, Michel, please understand that I will always hold you dear to me above all others. Life has kept us apart, but not in my heart.

There is much talk wherever I go that there might be a war. But why should there be war? I do worry about you so, Michel. Robert's father and brother are both in the army as well, so there is no escaping it, I suppose. Fortunately, England seems somehow detached from what is happening on the continent.

The wedding will be in Essex in the fall and, of course, you will be invited, but I will understand if you choose not to come.

I will always love you and treasure our memories together. Forgive me for wanting something other than our love.

—Camille

PART III

▼

CHAPTER 16

▼

Valcourt, June, 1917

...Hail litters over Mary there not here just give them what's morphine the matter with these lights my god take that one to bandages nurse theatre immediately no, not that one the one with the full of grace there's an officer here what the hell difference does my god pull that tourniquet Allah is there but great over here with that one his pulse is weakening what have we got chest shrapnel here head his pupil is dilating trepan set to me chest drain alcohols swab Hail Father Mary if you'll stop for a moment light over here scalpel to me now scalpel to me...

CHAPTER 17

▼

"It is best, if you try not to speak. You know, I ran into Lefevre at the train station. Yes, and he said that they're going to promote you. To Major. Yes. I heard they evacuated Rennaut to Paris last night. His leg was pretty bad but they say he'll pull through. Mansour was not so lucky. Died of his chest wound when the dugout beams collapsed. Peaceful though. Lots of morphine I suppose. Well, the mutiny seems to have stopped. Back in the trenches for the moment at any rate. They've rounded up some of the leaders, I'm told. By the truck depot. Two are already sentenced for execution. A nasty business. Nasty business…Well, it's almost daybreak now. You'll need your rest. You know that beam in the dugout that crushed Mansour was meant for me. Oh yes, he saved my life and yours. An old, dried-up priest, hardly fit for giving the last sacraments. But all those dead and dying boys in the field. Muslim, German, French—I couldn't tell with their bodies shattered and faces shot off. I suppose there have always been wars. My father was a soldier, you know. Yes, I still have his cavalry sword. Seems somehow quaint doesn't it, I mean cavalry in this age of machineguns and airplanes dropping bombs. But all those artillery shells exploding all around. The sound. I'll never forget it. The ground trembling with fear. At the same time, there is a kind of awe one feels, like being in the presence of God's wrath. A terrible beauty. It's the awe in the face of evil. But are our French guns evil, too, or just the Germans'? They are Christians, too. Catholics even. The Bavarian regiment we fought were all Catholics, it seems. I found their communion papers stained in blood in their uniforms. Same God, same church, same grip on madness. But the sound of the shells; it affected me somehow. What could I do? Too caught up in my own fear even to really be of proper help to them. Father Maigret would have done a proper job of giving last rites. Yes, death is a young man's game. You still have that certainty. That confidence. I'm too old to respect it. Too many doubts. Seen too much of this world perhaps. Sometimes I feel I'd welcome death. But what could I do when they called me out of retirement. Retirement, yes. A small cottage with only the geraniums to water. Tea with Mrs. Ornier. The twice yearly visit of the bishop who loved his cakes. Who among us could have dreamed the Germans would attack a place such as Valcourt. Such a tiny place really. A few farmers, a baker, an abbey, and not much else, and yet there are hundreds of dead in the fields. Guts and legs and heads and shoes and the pictures of their mothers. And that smell. You never forget it. All over the fields they are and by the river. Oh yes, I would play by the river. That stretch of the river by the willows. After school we would fish or throw rocks at the geese. And meet the girls there…I was a devilish little boy…Hardly knew anything. Anything, but a simple joy. A small place, really. Well, I almost forgot, a corporal whose name escapes me, wanted you to have this. I'll just put it here on the nightstand. His Koran, you see. He wanted you to have it. He…he gave it to me right before he died. Funny how he seemed to know which breath would be his last. Yes, and by some miracle the windows survived. Undamaged through it all. A thousand bodies strewn in front of them. Like a sacrifice before an altar, I suppose. But anyway, I brought a small gift for you as well. When your up to it, of course."

Dierot delicately placed the small wooden box that held a set of watercolors on the small nightstand by the bed and then positioned the Koran on the top.

CHAPTER 18

▼

In May 1917, during a lull in the springtime fighting, the Duchess of Aurteuil casually mentioned to Colonel Lefevre at a Parisian bridge party that her summer home and grounds might possibly be used to temporarily house a few wounded officers from "the right families." Neither she nor the French High Command had anticipated an imminent German offensive of three full battalions fifteen kilometers from her estate. When the large general hospitals in Paris were overwhelmed with casualties from Verdun, her chateau at Beaumontre was rapidly converted into a field hospital. Within three days of the battle at Valcourt, thirty-six men, eight wounded officers from the 3d Moroccan battalion and two German officers were transferred to Beaumontre. Two days later, four nurses and one physician from the American Hospital in Paris arrived to assist the single French surgeon on duty. The baroque ballroom in the east wing served as the main ward for the enlisted men and its adjoining central kitchen was converted into an operating theatre. The ballroom, with its inlaid cherry floor, gilded Corinthian columns, and turquoise ceiling had not been used since the marriage of the duchess's daughter some twelve years before. Beds for the officers were set up in the west wing of the house in the drawing room next to the library. A sentry with his rifle stood guard at the entrance to a short corridor that connected the drawing room to a glass and wrought iron orangerie that held a single wounded soldier felt to be one of the leaders of the mutiny.

Shortly after 9:00 PM, the American nurse taking Hassan's rapid pulse noticed some stirring from the French officer as he violently turned his shoulders and moaned. She hurried to the east wing and retrieved Captain Wilkerson Lewis, the

American surgeon on night duty, who was drinking coffee in the servant quarters adjacent to the kitchen.

Lewis lifted up the handwritten chart at the foot of Hassan's bed and translated the French medical history as best he could. He read quietly out loud to himself, "Captain, 3d Moroccan. Wounded three days ago at Valcourt. Depressed skull fracture, collapsed lung, multiple rib fractures, and deep left thigh laceration. Trepanned at 1700 hours on the seventeenth by Lebrun. Post-operative day five, chest drainage tube with stable output of 200 ml per shift. Scheduled for debridement and closure of thigh wound tomorrow morning." Lewis then sensed the presence of someone behind him and turned expecting to find the nurse. Instead he found a small, brown-skinned soldier holding a leather satchel under his arm.

"Excuse me, corporal, may I help you?" asked Lewis.

"You see, doctor, we pulled him out," the soldier replied.

"I'm not sure I understand," replied Lewis.

"Captain Hassan, sir. His dugout took a direct hit, sir. The boys and I dug him out. And we got the priest and Mansour, too, sir. We used our helmets and then our bare hands, sir. Don't know how we got the strength to do it, sir."

Looking at the diminutive man in the shadows, Lewis said, "Yes, now I see, corporal. Although I don't know anything about a priest or a soldier named Mansour."

"Will he live doctor—Captain Hassan?"

"A bit too early to tell, I suspect. Head and chest wounds are the most serious. But we'll do our best."

"Yes, sir. But I came to bring this, sir. We found some of his pictures, sir." The soldier handed the leather satchel over to Lewis.

"Yes, I'm sure he'll be grateful for these, corporal. Corporal...?"

"Corporal Sayed, sir."

After being on duty for nearly seventy-two hours, after rounds that evening with the nurses, Lewis collapsed from exhaustion in a leather chair in the library. Its high ceiling, paneled walls with burled oak and Venetian chandelier were echoes of forgotten age. Lewis thought to himself, taking stock of the situation, "My God, half these patients need complicated surgery. Even if I knew how to do these operations, we don't have enough supplies or anesthetics to cope with any of this. Probably the same with every hospital in Paris though. How do you deal with three thousand casualties a day?" He then realized, "This opulent mansion, reminds me of something out of Newport. But it's going to be a damned mansion of death unless I get more help."

Distracted, he leafed slowly though the leather satchel Sayed had given him. He found a dozen or more watercolors, various ink sketches, and a small oil painting with a simple wood frame. The watercolors were all portraits of the Arab soldiers in Hassan's battalion. Lewis was struck by how the modernist style reflected a depth of emotion in the brown faces and dark eyes of the men. He found them merely curious at first, but upon further reflection Lewis felt as if he noticed something deeper, an undefined resonance and went back more slowly over the paintings. A connection in their emotions began to emerge. At first he could not place where he had seen it before. He certainly had not encountered it among his French patients in the hospitals in Paris, or in his boyhood growing up among the fishermen of coastal Maine. As he continued to turn through the portraits, however, memories of his ward patients during his internship at Bellevue Hospital suddenly came to mind. He recognized the look of the immigrants he had treated. A shared look, not one of defeat or defiance, but a look reflecting an acceptance of a difficult lot in life. No one forced them to get on a boat from Dublin or Genoa or Hamburg. No one handed them a fortune or the keys to New York City, only a promissory note of a better life they would have to create on their own. Most importantly, they had found in the New World a community of people who also spoke German or Italian or Polish and they would struggle together. Lewis remembered how they crammed the hallways and waiting rooms of the hospital to hear of any news about their friends or loved ones. That community was somehow a shared hope in the future, if not for themselves, then possibly for their children. Perhaps Hassan had sensed that connection in these men, outsiders from a different continent and different culture, but with some deeper sense of unity.

As he continued to pour through Hassan's work, another aspect of the portraits stuck in Lewis's mind. They were painted in a curious and unfamiliar style that he could not quite place. On his weekends off, he had strolled through the Parisian galleries more curious than anything else. Although to a degree the portraits were representational and realistic, the faces were more angular and seemingly two-dimensional, almost in a way to Lewis like the icons he had seen in the Catholic churches in Portland. The edges of the portraits framed in black were combined with subtle light and shadow. It was a style unlike anything he had seen before—subtle but somehow provocative.

The eight sketches appeared all to be of the same subject, a partially destroyed church with only one wall standing. The wall and an adjacent pile of stones were done abstractly in ink and charcoal. In the center of the wall was a stained glass window painted with intensely brilliant colors. Lewis had not seen such deep hues of red, green, and blue done in watercolors.

The small oil painting was quite different from the other work and not in a modernist style. It was a remarkably lifelike portrait of an old man working in a garden next to a stone fence. His chapeau was slightly crooked with his weathered hands resting on a shovel. His brown eyes reflected an unmistakable tenderness. Lewis was curious about the two spires meticulously depicted in the distant background.

Lewis's study of the painting was interrupted by a nurse rushing into the room, "He's spiked a high fever again, Doctor."

For two days, Hassan had nightly fevers of 103. Lewis had been worried at first that he was developing meningitis from the trepanning. Hassan, however, seemed to be improving neurologically, with only minimal residual arm and leg weakness. After repeating his physical examination, however, the cause for the fever became all too evident. Pus was leaking around the chest drain, and the skin over his lower chest wall was markedly red and indurated. "Empyema, of course. There must have been bits of clothing or shrapnel in the chest wound. Why didn't I think of that sooner?"

His only chance now was to operate and remove the infected clot around Hassan's lung before he developed septicemia or a fatal pneumonia. Lewis felt Hassan's pulse weakening as he turned from side to side and spoke unintelligibly over and over in his febrile state. Lewis now knew that Hassan needed urgent surgery and that there was only one surgeon who could pull it off. "I've got to get Morrissey to do this," he said to himself.

Captain Lewis had one additional year of training in general surgery after his rotating internship at the Cleveland Clinic. Although as an intern he had assisted in thoracic surgery on the TB wards, he certainly did not feel comfortable doing this extensive an operation on his own with just a nurse to give the ether anesthesia. He placed a call to Colonel James Morrissey at the American Hospital in Paris. The return call came later that night.

"Wilk, what's the hell's going on up there? Speak fast, man, I've got a ton surgical cases this week."

"Colonel, I've got a tough thoracic case only you can do, sir. A French officer with an empyema. Probably needs a rib resection and a decortication. Thing is, sir, he's getting septic."

"I see. All right, got my schedule book here. Let's see, tomorrow is Thursday. OK Wilk, you get him down here tomorrow midmorning. I'll move things around and try somehow to work him in sometime in the afternoon. Just make sure you keep up with his fluids until then."

"Yes, sir. By the way something you might find interesting, sir. He's a modern artist, sir. Or at least that's how I think you would classify him. I'll bring some of his paintings along. You'll find them interesting."

"Well, I'll be damned. What's his name?"

"Hassan, sir, from the Moroccan battalion. He's half-French, so they say. Those Arab boys got pretty badly chewed up by the Kraut offensive. Fifty percent casualties and the mutiny and all. But the line still held."

"Hassan, eh. Well, I don't think he's famous yet, thank God. A potential new discovery. That's how I like it. Once these fellas sell two sketches they become damned insufferable. Well, duty calls. You get that officer down here and we'll patch him up, Wilk."

Colonel James Madison Morrissey, MD, had come from a distinguished Pittsburgh banking family and had been the heir apparent to Dr. Wilson Lattimore's surgical practice at the Massachusetts General Hospital. An incident occurred, however, near the time of Dr. Lattimore's retirement. Some said it was between Morrissey and Lattimore's daughter, but others did not know the precise circumstances. In any event, Morrissey, a hard-drinking Irish Catholic became a most unlikely Lutheran medical missionary. He immediately left for China and remained in Shanghai for six years until the outbreak of the war.

Shortly after arriving in Paris two years ago, Morrissey purchased a large home in Clichy, a "romantic" house, according to the real estate agent, with its graceful gardens, stately oaks, and high iron fences. Its greatest appeal for Morrissey, however, was the unusually large size and ample lighting of the drawing rooms, which enabled him to display his impressive collection of modern paintings. Most weekday nights he slept on the battered leather couch, bottle in hand, in the American Hospital solarium next to his surgical ward. His curly yellow hair and mustache always needed trimming and his white coat was often disheveled from sleeping in his clothes. Yet Morrissey practiced strict hygiene and formality on his ward rounds. Failure to wash one's hands or give proper respect to patients or nurses was met with a swift reprimand. Morrissey was a medical contrarian and felt that much of current surgical practice was no more beneficial than witchcraft or alchemy. In many instances, Morrissey espoused the heretical view that the prudent thing was in fact, not to operate. "Don't cut unless you are certain to drain pus or stop bleeding!" was his constant refrain to the junior doctors. When an operation was required, it must be accomplished swiftly with an economy of dissection in order to minimize the spread of infection and reduce the length of the ether anesthetic.

Lewis had spent six months of additional training on Morrissey's ward service and greatly improved his operative skills at the American Hospital. After several years and numerous operative triumphs, Morrissey's reputation as a surgeon and iconoclast spread throughout all of Paris. He was alternatively famous or notorious among his peers, who jealously marveled at the wide scope of technically difficult operations he had mastered, performing neurosurgical, thoracic, and abdominal operations with equal dexterity. Amputations and orthopedics, as Morrissey often noted, were, however, best left to "out-of-work carpenters."

Lebrun, the French surgeon, reported back to Beaumontre from leave at 7:00 AM on Thursday morning. Lewis himself accompanied Hassan in an American Field Service Model T ambulance on the three-hour trip to Paris. His condition was clearly worsening at one point, with his blood pressure falling and his pulse racing, and Lewis held off on the morphine when his pulsed weakened, which only increased Hassan's agony. As they pulled into the semicircular stone driveway of the American Hospital, Lewis saw the familiar crumpled white coat of Morrissey smoking a cigarette on the steps of the imposing Georgian red brick building.

"Wilk, listen: I want you to scrub in with me. OR 11. Your old stomping grounds. Can't trust these French juniors to give me decent exposure. Just take him right up to pre-op. We're nearly ready to go."

Within thirty minutes, Lewis had scrubbed in and was assisting Morrissey. After personally administering the ether anesthetic, Morrissey made a long intercostal incision over the infected site, resected the adjacent rib, and carefully evacuated the gelatinous infected clot from the pleural space round Hassan's collapsed lung. The malodorous smell of the liquefied pus was so intense that Lewis had to excuse himself and put cologne water on his mask in order to continue. Near the end of the surgery, they sewed in a large chest tube for drainage and transported Hassan to a ward bed right next to the solarium where Morrissey slept. Hassan's pulse waxed and waned throughout the night and Morrissey did not sleep until the crisis had passed.

Within days the thoracic infection gradually cleared after surgery. His thigh wound was debrided two days later and also began to heal. Over the next ten days Hassan's strength and overall condition improved steadily. Much to the dismay of the nursing staff, he began to try to walk the long dimly lit corridors at all hours with his cane still adjusting to a mild weakness on his left side from the lingering effects of the subdural hematoma. His telegram to Colonel Lefevre requesting to return to active duty was politely declined and he was assigned to six months medical leave. The first three months of which could be spent rehabilitating at the Beaumontre chateau with other men from his regiment. He soon was well enough to insist on leaving Paris.

Upon hearing of Hassan's planned departure back north, Morrissey stopped him in the hallway, noting, "You can't go back without coming to my party tonight. Lewis took the liberty of showing me some of your work. Remarkable in many respects. I particularly like the sketches of the ruined church."

"The abbey, yes. Then you shall have one," replied Hassan.

CHAPTER 19

▼

Without family or social ambitions, Colonel Morrissey's limited waking moments outside the American Hospital were spent pursuing his two other great passions, microbiology and modern art. His small private fortune funded several research endeavors at the Pasteur Institute and gained him access to their twice monthly research "teas." Morrissey managed to enliven these solemn affairs with his controversial views fortified by liberal doses of champagne for all. On more than one occasion, however, Morrissey lost patience with the academic train of the discussion, always striving for further subclassification of all known bacteria. He was often known to end the evening with the raucous refrain, "I don't want to name these bugs any more, Goddamn it; I just want to kill them!"

Every two or three months Morrissey would ring up his English valet from the hospital on Friday night with the instructions, "Owen, let's have a party on Saturday night. Tell Maggie to fix something up. Invite all the regulars and scrounge up a few more interesting characters. I'll be home Saturday afternoon after I make my rounds of the galleries."

In fact, there was never a guest list for Morrissey's soirees. Owen gave up on that score after two failed attempts that produced mostly stuffy socialites and few of the artists Morrissey found interesting. A more effective approach Owen found was for him to discretely "put the word out" at a few avant-garde galleries in Montparnasse and Montmartre. Without fail, a mélange of artists, models, writers, expatriate hangers-on, and gallery owners would materialize for the free buffet and open bar. Although many of the bohemian guests claimed their motivation to attend Morrissey's parties was primarily for the free food and liquor, a more subtle reason was to observe the newest paintings Morrissey had purchased and placed on display in his rambling mansion. For many of the artists, critiquing the latest art works hung in leading Parisian galleries was an enjoyable aesthetic pastime, but seeing what styles devotees such as Morrissey actually purchased was an economic necessity.

On the afternoon before the event, Owen had four local workmen remove all the downstairs furniture and oriental rugs and place them in the carriage house behind the garden. As Owen had observed, removing the furniture not only saved them from the inevitable spills and wear and tear, but the lack of a comfortable place to sit tended to minimize the chance that the party would go on late after midnight.

The setup for Morrissey's parties was always the same. The center leaves were inserted into the long oak dining table and taken into the drawing room for the buffet. In the opposite corner, a heavy cherry drop-leaf table served as the bar. Adjacent to the bar was another smaller oak table with a green velvet cloth and a microscope.

Morrissey took a tiny clump of dirt from his compost garden, mixed it with a bit of pond water, and placed it under a glass slide cover. The house rule was that in order to take a free drink each guest was required to look first through the microscope at the primordial microbes in the garden dirt.

Whenever a neophyte was introduced to this ritual, Morrissey in his booming baritone would remark for all to hear "Take notice, all you so-called modern artists striving for a new vision of the world. There is a universe right here in this pond scum more vibrant and complex than you can possibly imagine!"

Then Morrissey would show them slides of the microorganisms that he had carefully prepared with various colored stains of intense reds, blues, and greens. The painters and sculptors peering at the myriad of multicolored bacteria and fungi sighed in wonder at the loveliness of the microbial world. At the evening's midpoint, Morrissey would inevitably exclaim, "You now can appreciate the splendor of our natural world in the smallest of things. Science can teach you a new way of seeing. So be open to its ideas wherever the source, all of you."

The point for Morrissey was not to highlight the esoteric science of the Pasteur Institute, but to provocatively introduce them to a world beyond the narrow prism of their café society. This was a society that had in many instances managed to block out any thought of the brutal war being fought a few hours away.

After the encounter with the microscope, the newly christened guests were free to eat and drink and take in Morrissey's remarkable art collection. The pale yellow drawing room walls illuminated by a series of gas-lit sconces functioned as the main gallery for Morrissey's latest acquisitions. The upstairs library and sitting room housed the more "permanent collection" that Morrissey had not yet sold to visiting American collectors or museums in New York, Boston, or Baltimore.

That Saturday evening the guests arriving at 7:00 PM took in the latest works by Matisse, Derain, Braque, and Picasso prominently featured in the drawing room. Hassan's work of the abbey was also on display and generated much interest, as it was unsigned. By 9:00 PM, when Hassan arrived, the house was overflowing with a raucous crowd.

Morrissey met him on the steps and shook his hand warmly, "Glad you could make it. You look remarkably well, Major. I'm hoping Braque will arrive a bit later. One bit of irony is that you both had similar head injuries. But enough of those unpleasant memories. I've taken the liberty of displaying your painting downstairs if you don't mind. You'll see it over there. But first I want to get your impressions of my collection."

"Thank you, Colonel; you've saved my life and have been most kind, but I came primarily to thank you for my recovery and only stay a moment. Captain Lewis and I will be heading back to Beaumontre and the regiment early tomorrow morning, to finally see the men again."

As he was still slightly unsteady with his cane, Morrissey discreetly took hold of Hassan's elbow and walked him around the perimeter of the crowed room. He stopped before his newest Braque, a collage of a guitar done in charcoal with overlaid strips of painted paper.

Morrissey began, "Subdued yet stimulating, isn't it? Perhaps not as revolutionary as his highly fragmented landscapes a few years ago at l'Etaque. But still, the intersection and overlaying of multiple planes draws the object nearer in some way, doesn't it? The multiple perspectives are quite striking. A way of seeing the world freed from the constraints of a single vanishing point or line of sight. We're finally free from the Renaissance."

"Indeed," a deep voice from behind them replied. "But I prefer to think of the fragmentation more as a metaphor. A metaphor for modernity."

They turned around and Morrissey half laughingly said, "Carvalho, how very nice to see you. Let me introduce Major Hassan—as capable an artist as a soldier, as you'll see from the sketch on display over there."

As Hassan and Carvalho embraced, Carvalho said excitedly, "Oh, we are old friends, Colonel, old friends indeed."

"How extraordinary," replied Morrissey.

"Yes, Michel was my pupil many years ago, but I perhaps learned more from him than he realized. How are you, my boy? I can see you have been wounded, but what are you painting these days?"

Michel and Carvalho went off into a corner and spent hours catching up on their divergent lives. Near the end of the evening, Morrissey spoke in private to Michel just as Carvalho was leaving.

"Please come join me, Major, for a night cap. You know that the nature of your injury is such that it will be impossible for you to go back to active duty. I've already signed the necessary paperwork for your medical discharge if you choose it. Oh, I'm sure the army might have a desk job for you somewhere, but my guess is that you may wish to continue your painting."

"Perhaps you are right, Colonel. The problem is that, at the moment, I find it impossible to think of painting as having any meaning at all. I do feel the need to paint from time to time, but somehow since my surgery I don't seem able to pick up a brush."

"I can appreciate that, and I'm also aware that what passes for art these days in Paris is either chauvinistic propaganda or a hundred cheap cubists' imitations of Picasso or Braque. But perhaps let me make a suggestion. There is a small, but very original group of artists in Zurich at the moment. My friend Hans Arp is there and I understand they have just opened a gallery. More to the point, Carvalho here has told me of an exhibition at the gallery in Zurich in few weeks' time that I think you should attend. You see, I want you to find out if, in your opinion, this new school of art is not just a fad, but worthy of my modern art collection. Would you consider it?"

"Perhaps. I will think about it and let you know. I haven't even been officially discharged yet, but perhaps you're right. I feel I need a change as well, but I must first say good-bye to old friends."

CHAPTER 20

▼

The massive carved doors of the rectory were unlocked and, hearing no reply to his inquiry, Michel struggled with his cane to walk down the darkened corridor to the one room with a light under its door. A familiar smell came over him as he proceeded in the dimmed morning light. The stagnant air reminded him of the tool shed the first thing in the morning before Tommasso would open the clapboard door to the sunlight. Hassan knocked on the door at 8:00 AM and, as he entered, he saw Father Dierot standing on a stool taking down a large glass covered display of butterflies.

"Careful, Father, let me help you," Michel said as he gently helped lower the large case.

"Oh, Major Hassan, how good of you to come. So you got my message."

"Yes, I should have come by earlier but I'm just back from the hospital. I have come to say good-bye, Father, and to thank you. I thank you for the courage you showed in helping the men."

"Yes, well, I should be the one thanking you and your men, Major. We might be conversing in German at the moment if not for your real courage. My actions only got in the way, I suppose, but that's just part of the job. By the way, Major, I shall also be saying my good-byes. My retirement has been reinstated, so to speak. A new young man will be taking over the parish in a few days. So I'm just clearing out at the moment. These butterflies. Do you like butterflies, Major?"

"I only can appreciate that they are very beautiful. Almost unnaturally so with their brilliant colors."

"Yes, it's the colors that are so seductive, aren't they? But this one here. If I plopped him down in a field of sunflowers you'd have a devil of a time finding him. Or this one. Try finding this one on a poplar leaf. Yes, nature has its beauty and its purposes. Please sit down, Major."

They sat for a moment in silence and then Dierot said, "You know, before my knees went bad, that was one of my favorite pastimes on a summer afternoon, catching butterflies, that is. All seven of these cases up here are mine. Started as a boy, you know. Ah, fortunately it seems the local naturalist society has a place for them. At least the rare ones. It's just a matter of carting them down there. That way I will still get to see them when I attend the naturalist society lectures."

"And what does your study of nature teach us, Father, apart from nature's extraordinary palette of colors in its butterflies?"

"Oh many things, Major. Last week we had a lecture on the different functions of the thumb in apes and chimps. Fascinating to think about our human ancestry, isn't it? It really does seem that man is just a complicated ape."

"But an ape made in God's image, as they teach us."

"Yes. A divinely inspired ape, Major. One that has the capacity to create the stained glass windows in the abbey, but to destroy all the walls around it with a barrage of artillery shells. I was reading *Paris Soir* the other day. I was struck by a quote from someone close to Foch who claimed that this was the first war in human history to be global; a true world war, as they say. I find that observation somehow remarkable, don't you? My god, the thought that the first human endeavor that touches nearly all of mankind is a war. Well, I don't know what to think about our divinely inspired ape. A war whose origins are as obscure as its ending. A war that was supposed to be over in three months that has dragged out for three years. Oh well, at least we have the windows. It's comforting to know that with your talent, Major, you will be creating something of that inspired quality. Perhaps some place away from France, away from the war."

"Well, Father, that is my wish, too, but the fact is that I've have not been able to paint at the moment. The few times I've consciously tried to observe things my mind gets overwhelmed by other thoughts."

Father Dierot sat silently for a while and then offered, "Yes, I can quite understand. Some day, Major, we will rebuild the abbey. Some day when the war is over and just a bad dream. Some day."

"Yes, I hope for that time too, Father," Michel said as he slowly rose to leave. He limped badly as he approached the door.

"I see you're still using a cane, Major. Perhaps we all are still wounded in our own way."

Dierot then turned his gaze to the large windowsill and spoke softly, "It is said that identifying with Christ's passion on the cross is what heals us from the wounds of this sordid life. That is what the church would say, Major. But in my heart I would say that that is a mystery revealed to only a few. Yet I have seen with my own eyes the healing power of ordinary men and women through their selfless love for one another. That is no mystery requiring an act of faith, Major. That is a fact."

The two men sat in silence as the morning sunlight slowly filled the room.

"There is one piece of business that we need to discuss before you go, Major. A difficult business it seems, as it has to do with the mutiny. Most of the leaders of the mutiny were rounded up and shot right after the battle. Nine of them in fact from de Clairant's battalion alone. But one of the leaders, a sergeant in the artillery, was severely wounded and was not expected to live. Name of Mouton. I don't know if that name means anything to you. Anyway, he was sent to a hospital and somehow recovered. Well, it may be more precise to say that he has healed sufficiently to be able to be lined up against a garden wall and be shot. Although convicted by a military tribunal, he has appealed. Claims he didn't desert at all. The point is, Major, he claims you know him and has requested that you testify on his behalf at the appeal. This information was relayed to me by one of your Arab corporals. I forget his name. I spoke to Lefevre about the matter and said that you needn't trouble yourself about the appeal. It's an open-and-shut case apparently as the accused freely admits to being a leader of the mutiny. The thing that's curious to me is that most of the leaders of the mutiny were nowhere near the front lines when they were rounded up, but this man somehow managed to get himself shot up pretty badly."

"Mouton, you said. From the artillery. It's all been a blank to me, Father. Perhaps if I saw the man. Where is he now, Father?"

"Still at the chateau recovering from his injuries as far as I know. He'll be the one under guard. I guess he's sufficiently healed that the execution is scheduled to go forward immediately after the tribunal in the next few days. If you like, you may take my carriage." Dierot replied.

"Oh, one final thing, Major," replied Dierot as he pulled from a drawer a small leather-bound book. "A wounded German officer, I believe a captain, gave me this book at the dressing station just east of the abbey. He spoke perfect French to me before they gave him the morphine. I imagine he must have studied here, before the war. I had forgotten about it. One's emotions in those moments supplant one's memory, I suppose. You see, I'd forgotten about the book until I was cleaning out the place and discovered I'd put it in this drawer. I guess I thought it was his field manual or similar, but in fact it's a book of poetry. Mostly in German, but there are some splendid poems in French as well. There is a short one I particularly like. Permit me to read the few lines. It's entitled "Summer Storm in Normandy":

We walked along the endless rows
Of apple trees in June,
The blossoms almost past now,
With the first of summer's heat.
The straight lines of the orchard
Brought an order to the hillside.
We did not notice
The gathering clouds.
When you are young and in love,
You take little notice of nature's anger,
Preferring chance to logic.
But when the thunder shook the valley,
And the cool rain stung our faces,
We were grateful for the little shed.
We huddled there until the storm had passed.
The great scene playing out above us,
Nature's drama,
Caring little
For young lovers,
Or the falling apple blossoms.

Dierot then looked up at Michel, "I was just wondering, Major, if any of the German officers survived long enough to make it to Beaumontre."

"Yes, I do recall that there were two German officers under medical care at the chateau. Perhaps your poet was one of them. Wilkerson and LeBrun operated on both of them as I remember, but neither survived. I think your German officer wanted you to have that book and to read those poems, Father."

"Yes, I shall treasure them then. But tell me, Major, about the poem. The rain, the apple blossoms. Lately it preys upon my mind. Are we just the passive audience in some great drama like the two lovers in the summer storm? Is there no way to influence these forces?"

"I, for one, prefer to think there is, Father," Hassan replied. Then turning to leave, "Just not in the trenches, Father."

CHAPTER 21

▼

Hassan arrived at the chateau shortly after 11:00 AM. He remembered that there had been a single sentry on guard outside the orangerie adjacent to the main ward and he headed straight for there. The sentry rose from his chair and saluted as Hassan limped toward the sixteen-foot cherry door.

"Sir, on orders from Colonel Lefevre no one is allowed to…"

Hassan saluted and walked right past the sentry without replying. Entering the sunlit room he saw a man in the shadow of the single tapestry drape in a chair next to the bed starring at his chained hands. The man spoke first. "I didn't have high hopes that you would come, Captain, or I guess it's now Major."

Hassan responded, "Your name is Mouton?"

"Yes, Sergeant Arnaud Mouton, artillery battalion, Second Army. Do you not remember me? The horse-drawn company of 75's that I transferred to your command?"

Hassan took off his hat and placed it on a table near the man and sat down in a chair. "Yes, I remember you now. What happened that morning? The artillery battalion was to be put under de Clairant's command."

"What happened? Chaos. Most of the artillery officers including Legrange were killed in the opening barrage when a shell hit an ammunition dump. But the infantry battalion was worse off. Much worse. They panicked. Half of them ran. No one knew what to do until Nevers took charge."

"But de Clairant was in command."

Mouton stopped and looked out the window, with his right hand stroking the irons. He repositioned his elbow in the stained cloth sling and began again, "I was there Major. I saw Nevers take over. De Clairant panicked. Right in the middle of the German infantry attack after the barrage. He ran from the line. Yelling like a madman. Nevers pulled his revolver out and fired three times into the air. He rallied the troops and positioned our guns."

Hassan rose with a start.

Mouton continued, "I saw it, Major, with my own eyes. I was there. Nevers took over. He yelled at me and two corporals to position our guns right next to each other. We stacked all the battalion's guns together in the middle, wheel to wheel, all eighty guns. We held our fire until Germans reserves went over the top and then we blew them apart. At 400 yards. It was over in twenty minutes. The German batteries were starting to get a bead on us by the end, but it was too late for them. They had no infantry left. Nevers ordered us to disperse and asked for volunteers to go and support the Moroccans. That's when I came to you. 'Just go to the abbey,' Nevers said. 'Just go to the abbey and find Hassan.'"

"But de Clairant was in charge until the battle was almost over. That is what I've been told," Hassan shot back.

"That's not true, Major. I don't know how and when he was killed, but I do know I saw him desert in the line of duty at the critical moment, right when we needed him the most."

Hassan took the measure of the man in front of him: "Why should I believe you? They say you were a leader of the mutiny, a communist, and that you will be shot for it."

Mouton did not respond at first, but just fidgeted with his sling. He then began, "All that is true, Major, but I will not give them the satisfaction of calling me a deserter like de Clairant. It is also true that you were there, Major. You were there when I brought the guns. I kept firing until my company took a direct hit."

"Yes, and your artillery won the battle. That is also true."

"Then you will testify for me at the appeal, Major?"

"Yes."

"Then I must ask you one other favor. Sergeant Nevers was transferred to a hospital in Paris the day before my tribunal and couldn't testify. Something about an infected leg wound, they said, but I don't believe it. I don't think he was seriously wounded at all. He knows the whole story. If you could find him, it might change things. Major, we haven't much time. The appeal is set for nine o'clock tomorrow. The execution is to follow immediately. And they've been very secretive about where Nevers was sent. No one knows which hospital."

"You're right, Nevers is the key, and there isn't much time. Fortunately, I have some contacts in Paris who might prove useful. I will request a meeting with Lefevre tonight and insist upon a delay if necessary."

At noon, Hassan took the carriage and headed four miles south of Valcourt to Lefevre's headquarters at Chateau D'Amercy. Along the way, shafts of light broke though the ancient beeches; they rose and fell on the horse's neck like gentle waves creating a hypnotic effect. The war seemed for an instant very far away, even just a few miles from the front. A farmer stood leaning on his pitchfork and took a moment away from his hay to wave while a small boy raced alongside the stone fence paralleling the road. He shouted encouragement to the passing officer. The physical space in the green of that countryside surrounded him was a calm normalcy, but his thoughts soon turned to the mutiny, the battle, the trial, and the people it affected.

Upon entering the chateau he went straight to the communications center in the converted dining room. Although he had been to the chateau on only two other occasions, the corporal manning the telegraph wire immediately rose and saluted saying, "It is honor to be in your presence, Major."

"At ease, Corporal," replied Hassan. Taking a pen from the ink fountain, he hurriedly wrote a few lines and handed the paper to the corporal. "I want you to send this telegram right away to Colonel Morrissey at the American Hospital in Paris. Is that understood?"

"Clearly understood, Major."

"I'll be expecting a reply. So when you receive it, please notify me at once. I'll be back at Beaumontre later this afternoon. Now, if you wouldn't mind, would you please inform Colonel Lefevre that I wish to speak with him in private? It's about the appeal tomorrow."

"Right away, sir."

After a few minutes, Hassan was ushered into the grand dining room with two men sitting at he end of a long table.

Lefevre rose to speak, "Please join us for lunch, Major, we've barely started. Uh, let me introduce Captain Shoenburg from General Foch's command. He's a military lawyer and will be handling the official side, so to speak, of the appeal. I know you wished to speak with me alone about this matter, but in fact it might be very useful to include the Captain in our conversation if you don't mind."

"Very well. I shall decline your invitation for lunch as I think this will be a rather brief conversation. You see, I wish to speak at the appeal on behalf of the defendant."

Shoenburg interrupted at this point, "I gathered as much, Major. That, of course, is your prerogative as an officer. I should warn you somewhat delicately that your testimony will do no good. The facts in this case are incontrovertible. It could also prove to have other damaging effects on your future military career. That is, to be speaking on behalf of a deserter."

Hassan chose not to directly respond to Shoenburg and offered instead, "And there is someone else who might wish to testify, Sergeant Nevers from the 67th. I believe he may shed some light on the issue of the chain of command during the battle."

"I'm afraid that won't be possible, Major, as Nevers is now in Paris recovering from a leg wound. The appeal and then the execution are scheduled for eight o'clock tomorrow. There's simply not enough time for Nevers to get here."

"Then I must ask for a delay."

Shoenburg threw down his linen napkin and shouted back, "You're in no position to ask for anything, let alone an irrelevant witness from Paris."

"Then I must ask for a delay on the grounds that Mouton is still gravely ill and not recovered from his wounds," Hassan replied.

"He is sufficiently recovered from his wounds to be present and sitting on a chair to hear the verdict. By law, Mouton must be present and in the room when the sentence is handed out, but other than that, the state of his health is immaterial."

"I see then," Hassan shot back. "Tomorrow, gentlemen, at eight o'clock."

Hassan left the chateau and took the carriage back to Beaumontre and waited in his room for the telegram from Morrissey. It came earlier than expected: "FOUND NEVERS. PROCESSING PAPERWORK. WILL TAKE SEVERAL HOURS. WILL SEND IN MY CAR BUT EARLIEST HE CAN BE THERE IS NOON. MORRISSEY."

Father Dierot's diminutive fieldstone cottage seemed dwarfed by the rows of purple and blue foxglove shooting over its first floor window. Dierot was still there packing a few biology books when Hassan arrived at dusk. "I will need your help, father. My testimony on behalf of Mouton may not be decisive. It will not delay his execution. Nevers holds the key. The fact that they've sent him to Paris confirms it. I've managed to find him, but he will not be here before noon and Mouton will be executed by then. This is where you come to help mobilize the farmers. You must call a meeting in the town hall tonight and tell the farmers and villagers that the man who saved the stained glass windows in the abbey is being falsely accused of desertion. They must clog the road leading south of Valcourt with their carts and carriages and tractors to prevent Mouton from being delivered to the firing squad before noon."

"By God, Major, you're right. Consider it done!" exclaimed Dierot.

The bells from the Hotel de Ville tolled for over an hour as the villagers and farmers came in from the countryside and gradually assembled in the wooden pews to hear Dierot describe the situation. At dawn the next day, the Merton road was jammed with every conceivable vehicle available from a twenty-mile circumference. At 9:00 AM the Fiat military escort truck carrying Mouton and three guards came to a halt after they tried to push the carts and vehicles to the side. Sensing the futility of their efforts they returned to the chateau for reinforcements, but found that most of the men already on patrol and away from the grounds. This increased the delay and by 10:00, Lefevre, enraged by the intervention of the farmers, dispatched fifty soldiers in trucks to clear the road at all costs.

The gravel courtyard of Chateau D'Amercy was overflowing with farmers and their wives and children as they pressed against the rifle butts of the small military guard assigned to the firing squad. Inside at 12:30 PM, Mouton was seated, handcuffed in the drawing room of the mansion on a wooden chair directly opposite the tribunal. At least twenty soldiers from the 67th and Troisième sat on makeshift benches and dozens more crowed about in the hallway outside. Mouton did not recognize either Shoenburg or the two other senior officers sitting alongside Lefevre, but it became very clear after several exchanges that Captain Shoenburg was the one in charge. Hassan was allowed to testify first and, not seeing Nevers in the room, he tried to draw out his testimony. He began first with a prepared statement describing his meeting with de Clairant and the battle plan they agreed upon. He then proceeded to describe the battle scene before Mouton arrived and then described how the artillery company released from Nevers and the 67th destroyed the German infantry reserves. Hassan then followed up with a series of legal questions directed to Shoenburg about the precise military distinction between desertion and mutiny and their attendant penalties.

Openly exasperated with the last question, Lefevre rose to his feet and shouted, "That is enough, Major!"

A deep voice came from the rear of the room, "It is not quite, enough, Colonel." The words came from Sergeant Nevers in the back of the room as he strode to the front with no sign of a leg injury. The burly man took off his hat and placing it on a chair next to Hassan began, "I wish to address the tribunal in private, with only Major Hassan and the accused in the room."

Shoenburg spoke up loudly, "This is most unusual!"

Nevers rejoined, "What I have to say is most unusual!" Then in a muffled voice directed at Lefevre, "And I don't expect that the Colonel wants the world to hear it."

"Very well then," replied Lefevre. "Clear the room."

Nevers then began: "What I have to say is that man before you is no deserter. Sergeant Mouton, along with the soldiers of the artillery battalion, with great courage and skill under fire destroyed the German infantry reserves at the crucial moment of the battle. When I asked for volunteers, Mouton took twenty guns and quickly moved them a mile away to support the 3d Moroccans under Major Hassan."

Shoenburg began like a prosecutor trying to trip up a defendant in cross-examination, "But how could you have asked for volunteers, Sergeant? That would have been an act exceeding your authority. Captain de Clairant was still in charge at that time. The signed report I have in front of me that bears your name, Sergeant, says that Captain de Clairant directed the counterattack and was killed at the end of the battle when a shell hit his dugout."

Nevers knew at that point that the truth must come out. He looked down at his hands for a brief moment and then replied, "It is true I signed it, but it is a lie. I took over command after de Clairant panicked and deserted."

Lefevre then interrupted, "Liar!"

Nevers continued, "It's the truth, General. The other officers were killed and I took over. I somehow stabilized things, but by the time I found Captain de Clairant in the rear he was dead."

Shoenburg rose again and shouted in anger, "That can't be true. How could you know that?"

Nevers rose up in response, but then slowly sat back down and in a barely audible voice replied, "Because, because…I saw him shoot himself."

Then Nevers spoke directly to Lefevre, "Your nephew, not Mouton, deserted. The Boche used the oldest trick in the book. The opening barrage lasted over an hour. Then they stopped and we got out of our dugouts to take up our positions and the Germans immediately resumed the barrage again and blew apart the men in the front trenches. De Clairant panicked. He cracked. He ran screaming to the rear after five minutes of shelling. The lieutenants were all killed when the ammunition dump went up. I took over. I got control of things and positioned the artillery. We routed them. When it was over I asked for volunteers to go and help the Moroccans. Sergeant Mouton volunteered to go and lead a company to help Captain Hassan. I went to the communications trench to try and telegraph him and found de Clairant, your nephew, in a half-destroyed dugout in the rear. He was in a state. He was crying, pleading with me to shoot him. My God, how he looked! Eyes bloodied. He had scratched his face, his eyes, his neck. He was mad, I tell you. The clotted blood completely covered his face and neck and chest. Screaming he was. 'Shoot me, dear God,' he said. 'Shoot me!' I leaned over to help him get to his feet and he yanked my revolver out of my belt, but before I could stop him, he put it in his mouth and blew off his head."

Nevers struggled for a moment and then continued, "De Clairant fell back into the darkness. I pulled the pin on a hand grenade and blew up the bunker to make it look like he had been killed by enemy artillery."

A murmur rippled though the tribunal. Then Nevers continued, "I don't know about your definition of desertion, Colonel. But I know that this man, this man before you in chains, saved the lives of my battalion and the lives of Captain Hassan's battalion. There is a difference between mutiny and desertion."

Nevers leaned forward and directly looked into the eyes of the tribunal's officers, "And now I have a question for you, gentlemen. A question for all you majors and colonels fighting the war from the Chateau D'Amercy. Please answer me. Hasn't there been enough killing?"

Nothing was said. After several minutes, Shoenburg closed his large leather book with a deliberate act, pulled his chair back from the table, and left the room.

Sergeant Mouton was sentenced to three months of hard labor for passing out subversive pamphlets.

CHAPTER 22

▼

The stairs to Carvalho's studio seemed much steeper than Michel had remembered, and his ascent was made much more difficult by the large duffel bag on his shoulder. With modest financial success had come electric lights and a fresh coat of paint, but nothing else had changed. The door was still unlocked and the aroma of turpentine was just as off-putting as when he first walked into the studio fifteen years ago. Carvalho was standing on a small wooden stool engrossed in an enormous canvas.

Without turning around or stopping his work Carvalho said, "Wanting your old room back are you?" Then he gingerly stepped down and walked forward to embrace Hassan.

"Well, you're in luck. The boy I'm tutoring now is away for a few months. Another one of Victor's projects, it seems. A Portuguese. I don't know where in God's name Victor finds them, but, of course, he found you. He's not as passionate or talented as you, but then few ever are. How are you, my boy?"

"Recovering slowly, but recovering still. I am finished with the army, it seems, after all those years. It was good to see you looking so well at Morrissey's party. How are you?"

"Still arguing with Victor and still painting. That's what keeps my mind active. That much hasn't changed. Keeps us both engaged, I guess. The gallery is doing well enough, but Victor refuses to show any of the Futurists' or Expressionists' work, so I have to overrule him from time to time. With mixed results, of course. But wait a moment, Michel, there is a package and a letter that came for you over there on the table, forwarded from the regiment. And, of course, you can stay here as long as you need to sort yourself out. You look tired, Michel; I'll go fix us something to eat."

Michel sat down and opened the letter resting on top of a large package. It was from Rennaut telling him of his promotion to captain. His leg wound was still infected and the doctors feared the infection involved of the underlying shattered bone. He refused to stay any longer in the army convalescent hospital and after he was discharged left for Lyon to live with his mother. Fortunately, his pension as a captain was able to provide for his medical bills.

"I must get Dr. Morrissey to examine him if he is not better soon," Hassan thought to himself. He then turned to opening the large package neatly bound with brown paper and string. The package contained a large leather album containing many of his first watercolors painted at the orphanage. A letter was placed inside from Sister Esme.

CHAPTER 23

▼

Dear Michel,

I feel fortunate to have your forwarding address so I could be sure that you would receive this package. I hope in some small way the delight in seeing some of your earliest paintings again will diminish the sad news I have just received; Tommasso has died. A letter from his sister in Palermo came two weeks ago informing me of this. His sister explained that shortly before he died she had taken him on a journey to Syracuse to see a famous painting there. He said that you would understand and that he was at peace and prayed for your deliverance from this terrible war. He said that the happiest time of his life was working with you here at the orphanage.

Michel, in your sadness, I want to take heart in what Tommasso said and to believe in your God-given talent to create. The tragedy of this war cannot go on forever and soon I hope you will return to your life's work as a painter. You know how much I value art, especially religious art, but any art that you choose will be fulfilling as long as it comes directly from your true spirit. But let me tell you of one small fear that I have: that an artist such as you may become so isolated in the process of creation that he may lose the joy of life all around. Never be so consumed by your art that it creates no room for friends, love, and the appreciation for all that is good in this imperfect world.

With all my love and affection,
Sister Esme

Michel handed the letter to Carvalho and slowly slumped back into his chair. Carvalho said nothing but simply went over and put his arm around his shoulder. "You must sleep."

In the morning over coffee, Carvalho spoke to Michel: "I know how much you spoke of Tommasso that year you were my apprentice. You must not feel sorry for Tommasso. He knew that death is a part of life and had a good long life. Longer than most. More importantly, he found people and things in this life that he could truly love. Most of us never find even one person or thing that we love, but he found two of them. He loved his work, seeing beautiful things come forth from the soil in his garden, but more importantly, he loved you like a son. No, do not weep for Tommasso, just know that he found peace."

Michel, however, could not be consoled. "I never visited him when I had the chance. And now, he is gone."

"But he is not gone. Every single one of those watercolors you signed has 'for Tommasso' at the bottom. He is with you always in your heart, in your memory, and in those paintings."

Carvalho was silent for a while and then continued. "There's something I never told you, Michel, but now I feel that I must. When you first came to stay that night and became my pupil, did you notice something strange in the studio? Did you see that all but one or two paintings were wrapped up in burlap? Did you ever wonder at that? Well, the reason was that I thought I was finished. I convinced Victor that art was over for me and he agreed to sell all my paintings to collectors in America. Victor, you see, had arranged for them to be shipped the next day. I was dried up. Finished, I thought. I had always prided myself on my originality. Or what I thought was originality. I fancied myself as someone different. A trendsetter, someone able to change the visual vocabulary. I began to pay too much attention to the critics, and I started to value the new simply because no one had ever done it before, with no thought of the substance of what I was doing. But I knew deep down I had this sense, this deep sense, Michel, that I was a fraud. What I've come to learn is that we are all frauds in some way. The trick is to accept it and to feel humble for even a morsel of talent. But by that night when you came I had lost my edge. I was no longer producing novel work, or any works for that matter. But there you were. You came into the studio that night and I sensed in some small way that you believed in me. But there's something else. Do you remember telling me of Caravaggio and the artist who did the stained glass windows? There is nothing we do in this so-called modern art that can hold a candle to that! My God, the cavemen that picked up a smoldering charcoal and drew a water buffalo on their cave walls achieved more than all this cubist rubbish! So you see, Michel, you shocked me and challenged me, and saved me in way. I canceled the sale of those pictures the next day, much to Victor's distress. I put several of them where they belong, hanging in the cellar at Le Lapin Bleu! So look, what I'm saying is that we forget the truth. It is our fate. We have to reinvent it for every generation, but there is still nothing more true than the water buffalo or the medieval stained glass windows."

Later that morning Michel began walking in a light mist. His leg was still painful and unsteady and so he brought his cane. He wandered the streets and parks of Paris without any particular direction or purpose. Contained within his own thoughts, he was immune to the sounds and voices of the city straining to begin its day. It was strange at first to have no destination, to have nowhere to go and no compelling responsibilities. The last few years in the army he now realized had the effect of blunting his thoughts for the future and any concerns beyond the preparations of the battalion for the next day. Caught up in the war and the rigidity of the army, there was no time to think about himself. No one at the front could realistically think about the future. Michel had somehow always felt that Tommasso and Carvalho and his painting would always be there to sustain him. All that was called into question now. Suddenly given his freedom there was nothing he wanted to paint. It all seemed so trivial after all he had seen. It was just paint on a canvas—colors, light, and shade. It all hardly mattered after losing Tommasso.

He was unaware of how much time had gone by and seemed for a moment to lose his bearings until he looked up and saw a bridge across the Seine leading to Notre Dame Cathedral. It seemed hollow to him to go inside at first, a kind of betrayal, but he noticed his senses of sight and hearing suddenly became much more acute as he walked into the immense Gothic space.

There was a deep chord of resonant organ music for a brief moment and then whispering he could not understand. It soon became apparent that a wedding was taking place. It was a solemn affair with only the flat, atonal sound of the priest's muffled Latin filling the enormous space. The gray cloud cover prevented much natural light from entering the great windows. The flickering light of the dozens of candles near the altar only partially illuminated the ceremony as Michel rested and took a seat on a wooden chair in the back, carefully holding his officer's hat and cane in his lap.

Michel's mind drifted from fatigue, but he presently began to notice a murmur from a disturbance near the guests that he could not quite decipher. He then saw a young boy in gray shorts and a blue jacket, no more than fours years old, running up and down in the side aisle. His disapproving parents called to him repeatedly, but failed to restrain his boisterous movements as he hid behind the great stone pillars. The priest continued, but the child escaped several attempts of the seated guests to grab him in what seemed like a game of hide and seek. The murmurs continued and by this time the minor disturbance was something of an embarrassment for the scandalized onlookers.

Michel, however, instinctively saw the situation quite differently. Instead of being embarrassed by the animated child, he took a kind of delight in his vitality and youthful energy as well as the boy's unconscious defiance within the setting of strict limits and expectations. As the boy raced to the back of the pews, Michel extended his arms to him without realizing it. The boy suddenly stopped and stared at the shiny buttons on Michel's hat in his lap. Without hesitation, the boy simply climbed onto his lap and spent the next few minutes distracted and in a calm state of fascination with Michel's hat and epaulets. After the boy was quiet for several minutes, a grandmotherly figure emerged from the shadows to whisk him away with a slight, but noticeable nod to Michel in gratitude.

That night over dinner with Carvalho, Michel related the story of the young boy in the cathedral. In a way he could not explain that the experience had been uplifting. The contrast between the boy's energy and the static elegance and imposing space of the cathedral was hard to grasp at first, but Carvalho recognized it instantly.

"Life, living, breathing, loving, suffering. Man with all his evil and shortcomings has something stone and glass and paint on a canvass will never have. And that, dear Michel, is the point. Life will inevitably change, it will decay and die and we know it. We are aware of that limit to our time. To be an immortal like some mythological Zeus on Mount Olympus has no meaning. If things don't work out in this millennium, well there are always an infinite number of them left. That awareness of time—precious time and decay—is what gives every decision and everything we do meaning. That is why you must continue painting and being part of this world. Morrissey knows about these things. I would take his advice about Zurich. It is away from the war and there is new kind of art there."

PART IV

CHAPTER 24

▼

The watchtower's lone searchlight slowly scanned back and forth across the empty tracks illuminating only silvery particles of dust wafting in the locomotive's gray steam. A few indifferent bankers and businessmen queued in the long shadows of the station's Ionic pillars waiting to be cleared for the Zurich train. There seemed to Michel to be more military police on the platform than passengers. The young officer fidgeted with the collar of his ill-fitting uniform as he inspected Michel's papers. After several minutes, Michel offered politely, "May I suggest you look at the bottom of the second page."

"Oh yes, it says here, Major Michel Hassan, Second Army, honorably discharged, *blesse en guerre*. Right then, sir, all appears to be in order."

There were no other passengers in his small first-class compartment so Michel took out a wool sweater from his valise and used it as a pillow against the dusty window. He was exhausted by the series of trains and carriages from Paris and welcomed even a fitful sleep. Tomorrow he would be in Zurich, in a country whose soldiers lived above ground, wore skis, and protected pristine villages and farms, not in trenches dug into denuded landscapes.

This he knew was a self-imposed exile and he wanted to forget the past and live in a country not at war. He wanted to think about something other than writing letters to widows, or ammunition supplies, or coordinating with the artillery and even about the mutiny and the dishonor surrounding all aspects of it. Most of all he wanted to take stock of himself to realize what he had become and what he had lost. The war was all about loss: the loss of life, loss of innocence, loss of time, and loss of faith. He had lost the will to see things and to paint them. More importantly he had lost the emotional bonds that had moored his emotions for so long, the connections to Camille and Tommasso, Rennaut, and even Carvalho. Yet could those bonds be reformed?

Michel awoke at first light and peered out the window at an alpine universe that overwhelmed him by both its strangeness and majesty. The intensity of the light reflected off the snow was painful to his bloodshot eyes, a flat white veil without depth or shadow. This was not France and he knew it.

Michel had seen black-and-white photographs of the Alps, but his only real frame of reference had only been the barren battlegrounds of the western front and the wheat fields around Courville. He had never experienced a landscape on this scale, and the mountains seemed ten times taller than Chartres cathedral's spires. The serpentine train, silhouetted against the expanse of ice and rocks, strained in its slow descent. It seemed insignificant to Michel in comparison to its forbidding natural surrounding. He dozed off again, but when he later awoke the train slowly came to a halt at Zurich station.

Michel peered out from his compartment window at the vibrant and chaotic scene on the station tracks. Even at 7:00 AM the city's commercial life was in full force. The hawkers, cabbies, newspaper boys, and food vendors in their wool caps and woven vests were all vying for the attention of the suited business undertow washing though the Italianate marble floors of the Zurich terminal. Michel was startled to realize that there was no one at the station in uniform. The only visible police officer appeared more interested in the tobacco shop's cigar display than the small side-current and flotsam of drifters and pick pockets working over the morning commute. Michel put on his jacket, closed his valise, and, with cane in hand, made his way through the terminal. He was glad to be unnoticed and a stranger without a history. Even the guttural sounds of the German phases swirling around him were welcome. He had nothing against the German language; it seemed less pretentious than French, more the language of action, orders, and change. His leg was still quite stiff from the train ride, but as he passed a waste bin near the waiting cabs, he jettisoned his cane with a definitive gesture.

CHAPTER 25

▼

Zurich's social fabric in the winter of 1917 was one of disconnected castes. It was like the artisans and nobility in fourteenth-century Florence who lived in complete isolation on different floors of the same fortress-like palazzo. Physically separated by a ring of imposing mountains, Zurich was also psychologically isolated from Europe by its passion for Swiss neutrality. At the outset of the war, its German-speaking bourgeoisie politely cheered the Kaiser's initial victories in 1914 from the comfortable vantage of its sedate cafes much the same as one would cheer a good football result over a stein of beer. However, as the carnage mounted and gave way to the tragic death grip of the Western front, the conventional strand of Zurich society—its burghers, bankers, merchants, and ministers—slowly withdrew behind their comforting façade of compulsively swept sidewalks, moderately filled church pews, and well-scrubbed faces of its polite school children.

A clandestine, but tumultuous political dynamism, however, lay just beneath this surface of self-congratulatory materialism. During the war, Zurich's underground was rife with spies, deserters, arms dealers, anarchists, profiteers, revolutionaries, and communists from every corner of war-torn Europe. Their muted barroom conversations, back-alley graffiti, and late-night meetings in basement apartments went largely unnoticed beneath the commercial shroud of this most conventional of cities. Only a discarded anarchist poster, a rare arrest under questionable circumstances, or a radical manifesto left inadvertently on the chair at a café gave faint echoes of the political turmoil precipitated by the war.

Occupying a less visible stratum in Zurich's wartime cultural elite were such classically oriented, but innovative writers as James Joyce, Jorge Luis Borges, Hermann Hesse, Ranier Rilke, and Thomas Mann. They had come to Zurich to escape not only the chaos in Europe, but also the scrutiny of its city fathers. These literary refugees, in choosing a life of internal and contemplative exile, struggled to extend the limits of the old aesthetic order and create a new language and nexus of thought for an evolving and fragmented Industrial Age. The war for them was a tragic backdrop to be sure, but their art was not constructed as a reaction to the war or defined by the immediacy of its horror. Leopold Bloom could wander the streets of Dublin in a modern depiction of a Homeric quest, all played out in the course of a single day. Yet at the same time Joyce was writing, during a single day on the Somme a hundred thousand men would be incinerated in such a brutal and dehumanizing manner that no counterpart existed in the classic epics of warfare. From "The Iliad" to the "Song of Roland," conflict, military triumph, and defeat were central to the Western heroic tradition in the arts and poetry, but there was nothing heroic about mechanized butchery by faceless machineguns or artillery fire. Modernity with its new technology of dehumanizing warfare was best ignored if one still wished to cling to the humanistic tradition of Western letters.

In direct opposition to this cloistered elite was a countercurrent of radical artistic energy that began to clamor for recognition and visibility in wartime Zurich. This movement was fueled by an intense anger at the absurdity of the war and the deliberate subservience of "art" as propaganda. This backlash was led by a new generation of immigrant writers, painters, and poets who were disgusted at the acquiescence of the old order and totally rejected any marginal innovations in language or artistic form as hollow "modernism." For them the old rules and conventions from the Enlightenment onward were totally inadequate to express their outrage at Europe's maddening descent into barbarism. Their new art would not be disengaged like the narcissistic artists fleeing to Zurich to escape the war only to become cocooned in a self-referential sterility. No, their vitality in rejecting the old ideals would expose the decadence of a corrupt society, a society whose underlying hypocrisy and savagery were unmasked by the pointlessness of the war and the forces of aggressive nationalism it represented. It would embrace the irrationality of life rather than suppress or reject it. For these artists shock therapy and the complete destruction of the old artistic order was essential to recreate the groundwork for a new one. Art must be liberated from the stifling values of bourgeois materialism and the forces of tribalism masked as nationalistic pride that seemed unwilling or incapable of ending the war. The newly characterized unconscious mind and man's yearnings and desires were at their foundation, based on irrationality and chance. Art must reflect that truth. Neutral Zurich—prosperous, bourgeois, and disengaged—would unknowingly spawn this revolt.

In an unheated third floor walk-up flat in an alleyway off Spiegelstrasse, a small man with threadbare jacket and wool scarf rocked repetitively in a wooden chair to keep warm. His mornings were spent drinking strong black coffee and stroking his unruly goatee as he devoured smuggled Russian newspapers. Vladimir Ilyich Ulyanov, later known as Lenin, bided his time dreaming of the violent political spasm that would overthrow the czar. Just three doors down the alley, discarded multicolored flyers from freshly inked cubist woodcuts blew past the unlocked doorway of a converted beer hall. This nondescript tavern was soon to be the unlikely epicenter of its own revolution—a movement whose weapons of choice were poems and paintings not bayonets or bullets.

Hugo Ball, the movement's self-appointed impresario, fervently believed that a radically new artistic sensibility must be injected like a toxic drug into the stagnant circulation of the city with an aggression commensurate with the apathy of its citizenry. A complex, but disarming German émigré, he had personally selected the rundown bar in Zurich's bohemian quarter as the site for a new kind of performance art for the masses freed from the insularity of museums, the academy, and its parasitic art critics.

Hugo was perceptive enough, however, to understand the mentality of the debt-ridden tavern owner Jan. He made the case for the café's renovation not on the basis of a radical revolution in the arts, but as simply a better business proposition that would sell more sausages and beer. At first, the owner was having none of it, "Cabarets and showgirls are fine for Berlin and Paris, but this is Zurich. All the men here want with their beer is a bit of foam."

Ball had recently fled military conscription in Germany with a passport forged by his wife, Emmy. He had been the director of the experimental Expressionist theatre group at the Kammerspiele in Munich before escaping to Zurich. Having come this far he was not about to leave without closing the deal. With the large influx of both legal and illegal Germans in the past two years, Ball knew such a cabaret could potentially be a commercial success. Commercial success, however, was only of marginal interest to Ball. He was out for bigger game: to shock the entire art world through a seismic transformation right under the noses of the burghers of Zurich.

Ball was both persistent and persuasive: "But Jan, let me explain. There is absolutely no financial risk for you. We will do all the work in opening the cabaret, all the painting and the carpentry. And just think, Jan, how much more you can charge for the wine and liqueurs to all those new sophisticated tourists. Cabaret goers are wealthy and cosmopolitan, you know, and big tippers too. We'll give the cafe a new name; something exotic that will ring in their ears and pull them in. The place will be packed and then you won't be the owner of a rundown beer hall anymore."

"You're sure about this, these free-spending tourists or draft dodgers or whatever you like to call them."

"Absolutely, Jan! You see a little new paint over here, a stage over there, and beautiful Swiss maids delivering expensive wines and liqueurs to thirsty customers. A nice cabaret show to watch, a catchy new name for the place, and voilà: the cash register will be stuffed!"

"But, what name will you give this new cabaret, as you call it? Something solid and German I hope?

"Oh, no doubt, Jan. Solid and German. No doubt. We'll make Goethe proud!"

Within forty-eight hours, modernist woodcut posters by Marcel Slodki were tacked up all over the city proclaiming:

International Debut!

Cabaret Voltaire, #4 Spiegelstrasse

Seeks experimental artists, poets, musicians

For its gala opening, next Saturday

The first artist who walked into the cabaret that afternoon was Michel Hassan. The deceptive silence on the streets of the artist quarter and the distracted stares of the few pedestrians on Spiegelstrasse did not prepare him for the whirlwind scene inside. The Brownian motion of a dozen carpenters and painters shouting, hammering, and running around the cabaret created an impression of utter chaos. At the eye of the storm near the end of a partially built stage was a spindly man with thinning red hair and large round black reading glasses drooping down his nose. He was standing at a table flanked by papers piled up to his chest simultaneously shouting orders and invectives in German and French at no one in particular. He seemed like a conductor with the orchestra pit under revolt.

"Listen to me, comrades! Showtime is in two days whether you like it or not, damn it! And if we don't open, nobody gets paid!"

Michel ascended the makeshift stage and approached the man in command and, in his halting German offered, "Excuse me, I'm here looking for a painter. A man named Hans Arp. His landlady said he might be here."

The man answered back in perfect French.

"Hans yes, bravo! I'm Hugo Ball and over there somewhere is my wife, Emmy. Hans should be by later this afternoon. And who might you be?

"My name is Michel Hassan. I represent an art collector from Paris. I've been told that Hans and a group of artists in Zurich were forming a new school of art."

"Charming, but only partially correct," replied Hugo. "We are actually against all artistic schools or movements and against just about anything else the bourgeoisie stands for. We are for freedom in all its forms. Chance, randomness, the irrational. Both in the visual and performing arts." Then with a sweeping gesture of his arm extended outward toward the stage, Hugo continued, "Take these carpenters, for example; what's the chance they can meet a rational deadline. Anyway, glad you're here, Michel. It's encouraging that our meager attempts are being noticed in Paris. But creating a new kind of artistic freedom, as you say, is too limiting a description. We are creating a new artistic language right here, right now, in this rundown café. Don't you find that remarkable?"

"Yes, very much so."

"Good, then you must join us."

"Are you also a painter?" asked Michel.

"No, my interest is in words. Words freed from the prison of bourgeois linguistic forms. Poems in particular. Word poems. The poetry of sounds. Automatic language, free association, and so on. Perhaps now that I think of it, it's best if you take in some of the rehearsals tomorrow afternoon. See what it's all about. Assuming the stage is finished by then. As you can see, we are starting to put up a number of modern paintings and posters, but we have many more walls to fill to make this a gallery, an altar to a new art. But anyway, let me see now, I've got my list for the rehearsals here somewhere in one of these piles. Right, I'm actually on stage performing my sound poems just after Tzara and the Negro dancing, Act Four. If I can get my costume ready, that is. Be here, shall we say, three o'clock tomorrow. It will give you an idea of what the Voltaire is all about."

"That's fine, tomorrow then. But actually, I was wondering…you see, I'm between flats at the moment. Well, actually, I've just arrived, and I wondered if there was someone who might have a spare bedroom or a flat I could possibly share a room with."

"Oh, that's no problem. Hans has a huge flat, and his wife is out of town at the moment. I'm sure he'll put you up. Wait a moment; here he is by the door. Hans, over here, there's someone I want you to meet."

"Michel is from Paris. He's interested in our art. I was just saying it would be no problem for you to put him up for a while."

"Sure, Michel, come along. The wife is back visiting her mother for a few weeks, so I could use the company. I'm just heading back there now, so bring your gear. Rehearsals later this afternoon, right?" said Hans.

Hans Arp's "huge flat" was in reality, a cramped one-room flat overlooking a small square off Heigelstrasse. The toilet was down a dim narrow hallway and worked reluctantly. The hot water shower in the basement was similarly petulant and highly unpredictable. The furniture consisted of little more than two wooden chairs and a tattered sofa whose once scarlet crushed velvet was now nearly denuded with age and had the texture of Hans's three-day beard. The sofa simultaneously functioned as a kitchen table, repository of papers, art supply dispenser, and makeshift easel. Every inch of wall space appeared covered with art by Hans and his wife, Sophie, with dozens of other paintings stacked in untidy rows radiating out from the sofa like the exposed tree roots of a great oak.

"Please sit down and tell me about yourself," said Hans as he cleared away an armful of papers from the sofa.

Michel immediately noticed a very unusual small sculpture perhaps ten inches high precariously resting on the threadbare arm of the sofa. It was a figurine of a dancer with four arms delicately balanced on one foot. Michel stared at it quite closely for several moments, and then Hans explained, "Oh that's just something I picked up in an import store in Geneva. The dancing figure is the Hindu god Shiva."

Seeing a blank stare on Michel's face, he continued, "Shall I tell you about it? The genius of it is that Shiva is not only the god of destruction, but also the creator god who brings much goodness. The point of the dance is to bring everything in balance. Don't you think it's fascinating to have the same god destroying things and creating them at the same time? I'm going to give it to Tristan after he publishes his manifesto. I think it is right on the mark and captures in some way what we all are doing here. In a sense we must first destroy the old way of thinking so we can create a new art. Hopefully, a better, truer art, a more universal art."

Michel replied, "Interesting. Perhaps one should not underestimate the difficulties in the creation part of the story."

Hans replied, "That's true, and we shouldn't take ourselves so seriously to think that only this small band of artists here in Zurich can do it all, for God's sake. But we have to start somewhere and begin with new assumptions about art and the creative process. So much of our brain, our thinking, our lives—when you really consider it—is just left to chance. You're born into this family and not that family. You're French and so you fight the Germans, or so you're German and you fight the French. By accident you run into this woman and get married, but not to that other woman who you just missed meeting at the train station. You see?"

"I take it you don't care much for fate or 'God's divine hand' in all of this?" replied Michel.

"After this war? Let's just hope God didn't have a hand in it. No, I'm a believer in the random nature of things and creating an art that reflects that. In a way, that's what Hugo's sound poems are all about. Chance, and free association, are the key elements for their creation just like Freud uses free association in his psychotherapy. Hugo believes that journalism and the newspapers have corrupted our everyday language. The politicians use this language as well to serve their political ends. So in many ways our old language no longer conveys any true meaning. Listen, we don't want to miss the rehearsals. They are about to start in a half-hour. But this discussion is much more important. Let's have some more Riesling."

The two of them never made it to the rehearsals and talked nonstop about Michel's experience in the war and the new emerging art scene in Zurich. They drank cheap white wine all night and then slept until late in the afternoon. During their discussion, Hans explained to Michel the intriguing rivalries and strong personalities that were starting to appear in the nascent anti-art activities orbiting for several weeks around several galleries in Zurich. Ball was the self-appointed impresario and outward leader of the group. He was the driving force behind the renovation of the cabaret. The energetic and iconoclastic Romanian poet, Tristan Tzara, however, challenged Ball's dominance. Tzara had established himself as the group's theoretician, attempting to articulate the inherent contradictions of an art movement that was anti-art.

Hans explained that recently he felt a greater sense of importance in the work they were doing by creating a name and an identity for itself. All of these seemingly disparate anti-art activities could easily have been dismissed as trivial and inconsequential until the adoption of a name. That name was "Dada." This mere act of choosing a name had the effect of creating an identity of an actual "movement." Never mind the inherent contraction that Dada was fervently against all "movements" or systematic thought of any kind. It was fitting, if not characteristic, that even after the "Dada Manifesto" appeared no one really knew the derivation, meaning, or significance of the name Dada. Perhaps, as Hans said, that was precisely the point to distinguish themselves from other artists.

Some said the name Dada was chosen by chance by plunging a knife into a phone book. Others said it meant, "yes, yes" in Romanian. While others thought it meant a child's rocking horse in French or the tail of sacred cow in an African dialect. The main point was the name was deliciously and deliberately vague. Dada meant nothing in particular in every major language and, therefore, could not have the stifling suffix "ism" attached to it. Unlike mainstream movements, Dada sought to enrage, not seek the approval of, the bourgeois art world. It was not above selling a painting now and again to make ends meet.

Along with Tzara, another personality equally forceful and argumentative was the German medical student Richard Huelsenbeck. He and Ball made up the German contingent of Zurich Dada and sought to keep it in its purist combative form. Tzara, on the other hand, also valued the derisive feints of mocking humor rather than repetitive frontal assaults. Hans was a conciliator and felt he played an important role by staying out of these power struggles and diffusing the tension with the humor of his childish poems.

As soon as he awoke, Michel greeted Hans on the balcony. Hans was observing the street scene below and wrote down in a notebook every thought or association that came into his mind for an hour. This "automatic" writing extended over some ten pages. Hans then went inside, took a pair of dice, and rolled them on the table. The number six came up and he then meticulously circled each sixth word for the creation of his final poem.

As it turned out, there were no rehearsals that afternoon anyway as the cabaret stage was only half finished. Ball became so flustered that he threw up the huge stack of worker's inventories into the air in a dramatic gesture. He left in a rage, only to storm back in again an hour later proclaiming, "The show goes on as planned tomorrow at eight! We'll dance right on top of you bastards if you're not done by then! To hell with rehearsals; they take away all the spontaneity anyway! All power to the new!"

The Swiss carpenters and painters were desensitized to Ball's ranting by now. They did not even look up from their sawing and brushing to acknowledge this latest blustery threat. There was a remote chance the stage might actually be done by eight o'clock tomorrow and then they would be rid forever of this overbearing German.

The next night, the show went on at ten. The advertised international flavor of Dada was, in fact, correct with one exception; there was not one single Swiss participant. The walls of the bar and stage areas were entirely covered with modernist paintings and posters by Picasso, Janco, Arp, van Rees, and Segal. The audience was initially presented with nonsensical poems in Romanian and various African dialects by Tzara and then exotic Negro dances. A Russian émigré next sang music by Saint-Saëns. After each successive act, a few more members of the audience would trickle out. The reaction of the audience remaining at the end of the poem was stunned silence. This bewilderment only increased as Hans then leapt onto the stage, and in a serious, but slightly mocking tone recited his latest poem, "The Inconceivable Birth of Saint Kaspar":

No one there was alive that day to avoid seeing the miracle,
No one passed the collection plate to the elephants and railroad engineers who gazed in wonder,
At the empty crib where Kaspar didn't have his birth certificate,
Witnessed by the landlord who never cared for saints much anyway,
And left the party to have a beer with Father Christmas.
Alone, abandoned by the memory of invidious insects dreaming of revolt,
Against the indifference of a world without tulips.

Michel had been astounded and bewildered by the first few cabaret acts with the sound poems, the odd dances, and strange music. The overt irrationality of it all was jarring and seemingly pointless, but perhaps that was the idea after all. After all, what was "rational" about the war? For Michel, Han's poem changed everything. He found it absurdly humorous in a self-mocking way that punctured the seriousness of the whole affair. He laughed uncontrollably with each ponderously delivered line and felt a sense of release and joy; emotions he had rarely experienced in the years of the war.

At this point, the few stupefied customers still remaining in their seats didn't know whether to clap, call for the police, or demand their money back. They felt distressed that they had not come prepared with eggs or tomatoes. An initial wave of turbulent murmurings fluttered through the room. Soon there were sporadic outcries from the crowd. "Ridiculous! Clowns! Imposters!" The distressed owner, Jan, then rushed onto the stage to minimize the damage and with arms raised high, he shouted, "Free beer and sausages for everybody!"

Much later that evening when the patrons had long cleared out and the exhausted cleaning lady mindlessly swept the stage, Hans, Michel, and Hugo talked about the evening's performance with flat beer and high emotions.

Hugo began: "It was a success, I tell you! A true occasion to enrage the philistines. Did you see the look on the faces? Those cows! And they'll be back all right. They'll be back!"

"Yes, Hugo, if only to throw vegetables next time," quipped Hans.

"The chaos is the point, Hans. That's precisely the point."

"The critics will say that this is just a phase after the cubists and fauvists."

"To hell with the critics! Dada isn't some theoretical slab of ideas for sterile academic research. Dada is not a system. It's a state of mind! A state of rebellion!

And the freedom that comes when you tear down the gates. There are no rules when chance and sounds and random acts are employed to create art."

"I agree, but there's a fine line. Hugo, what do you say to the critics who argue that there is enough destruction in the world already without obliterating art and replacing it with some sort of anti-art? It seems distressingly to mirror the destruction of the war in some grotesque way," replied Hans.

"Not at all. The destruction of the propaganda that passes for so-called art all around us leads us to liberation. The liberation of sound from language, the liberation of painting from the canvas. The rage of Dada frees us. Just because Dada is not based on rationalism doesn't mean it's irrational. Sure it has no meaning in an absolute sense, but you tell me what does. Where the hell has Europe's grand experiment with rationalism taken us after all? Right into this war with all its chaos, I tell you. Look, Dada utterly rejects all the forces of nationalism and materialism that led to the war in the first place. Tristan and I will soon put something down on paper; perhaps publish our manifestoes, so you will see. The whole point is not some defined exercise so that critics can pontificate, but a new language, a new vision."

CHAPTER 26

▼

The gallery devoted to Dadaist paintings was in fact weeks away from opening, but Hugo had managed to talk to the director of Zurich's newly opened municipal museum into putting on a free show. The curator had been somewhat misled as to the content of the modernistic woodcuts and collages by Hugo's characterization of an "impressionistic flavor." With attendance flagging among the local burghers, the curator felt he had little to lose.

Hans and Michel were invited to preview the exhibition Saturday morning. Their footsteps echoed in unison as they walked up the marble stairway into a large atrium with a rotunda adorned with Greco-Roman murals.

"Impressive, in a Swiss sort of way," remarked Hans.

Yet as they walked into the first floor gallery it was clear that the newly open museum's permanent collection left much to be desired. A few third-rate English landscapes and forgettable Dutch still life paintings were scattered among some feeble representatives of the Renaissance. Worse was the fact that the laborers had been on strike until Friday and had barely begun to uncrate the Dadaist paintings.

"Well, we'll be in plenty of time for the tram," Michel said trying not to be overly disappointed.

"But as long as we're here, we might as well go upstairs. I think I hear some workmen. The stairwell is over there I believe."

As they ascended the stairs, muffled sounds of hammering could be heard as the workmen did the final adjustments for a painting newly purchased for the permanent collection. When they entered the second floor gallery, there were a number of smaller framed old masters, but at the end of the hall, an entire wall was taken up by a single large painting. The two workmen in overalls stood transfixed in front of it.

Hans was first to approach the painting and said only "remarkable" in a barely audible voice.

Although he had never seen a work by the painter, Michel intuitively knew him from Tommasso's description. "It's Caravaggio," said Michel. "I know it by the way he handles the darkness and the light and the intensity of the emotions."

The painting before them was Caravaggio's masterpiece "The Conversion of Saint Paul." It depicted Paul in his Roman tunic lying on the ground after having been violently thrown off his horse by the divine light of God's revelation. His arms are forcefully extended to the heavens and his eyes blinded by an ethereal amber light. This most Roman of Judea's citizens, Paul, had delighted in persecuting the early Christians. Now that man was lying helplessly supine on the road to Damascus. The light of Christ's forgiveness had transformed him for his sins. Much of the painting was in darkness except for the illuminated face of the new saint.

Michel now understood the intensity of Caravaggio's artistic vision. All the things that Tommasso had talked about now came back to him. The vast areas of shadows in the painting were striking in their own right. The darkness gave power and meaning to the light. Wasn't much of life given over to darkness anyway? The war, the empty feelings he carried inside, weren't these all manifestations of darkness as well? Caravaggio had been an outsider, always on the run and always aware of the presence of darkness. Was he not an outsider living in the shadows as well?

The four men stared at the painting without speaking. Finally after several minutes Hans spoke reverently, "There are some aspects of the older art that Dada must admit are worth saving. Things that speak to the heart and not the mind."

Late that afternoon over coffee in a café, Hans began by saying, "I could see you were as struck by the painting as I was. That kind of intensely human element, that emotional impact, is rare in art. Certainly nothing Dada has achieved captures that."

"I think you're right about that. Certainly what you all have been working to achieve has a different purpose, but it's almost playful by comparison," remarked Michel.

"I would say almost trivial in comparison. Dada is like some shiny pebble in a mountain stream that catches your eye for just a moment, and then you continue your hike through the woods. Or perhaps it is best thought of as an artistic 'sorbet,' something to cleanse the palate, but not of enough substance to be a proper course," said Hans.

"Maybe that's too harsh," Michel responded. "Conscious irrationality has its place, I suppose. The randomness of Dada art and in particular some of the pieces you have done, Hans, do reflect the random nature of life. It can be quite humorous when not taken too seriously. It's just that, for me, nothing can replace the power of human emotion."

"Yes, I understand that. But to really capture that requires a great artist, like Caravaggio, for example.

"Like Caravaggio."

PART V

▼

CHAPTER 27

▼

Dearest Michel,

Carvalho was good enough to give me your address and I feel that I must write to you. I do so hope that you are mending well in body and spirit and that the sojourn to Switzerland will enable you to find what you are looking for. Many of the children you played with here are now gone and news has just reached us that Paul and Jean-Luc both died at the front.

There is one particular tragedy among the many that I must share with you. Camille's husband, Robert, died of his wounds. Camille had been in England caring for Robert's brother Nigel, who was badly gassed at the front in Belgium. Sadly, he too died. Last week Camille returned to France and is staying with Madame Petrovski and I've asked her to help with the choir when she is able. Michel, I pray that you will send her some small note of consolation in her moment of great need. Hearing from you would provide much solace to Camille.

I will be frank with you, Michel, because it is the prerogative of an old woman weary of the sorrows of this world. Camille's marriage to Robert was undoubtedly a blow to you. We all knew of your love for her. But the ways of the heart are sometimes only understood by God and are often not fathomable by man. I have never doubted that she loved you as intensely as possible, but life has a way of unfolding in a pattern that does not always connect with our desires. Chance and fate intervene in random ways it seems. But one thing is certain; she has always cherished you and her love for you. It was you who brought her out of the wilderness of enmity and bitterness. Her love for you freed her from the haunting memory of her father and allowed her to pursue her great passion for singing. That passion took her away from you, but this was something she had to do. Her love for you, nonetheless, will endure as much as any great work of art. You must find it in yourself to forgive her. Forgiveness glances back charitably on the past, but gazes intently on the future. A future that holds the possibility of not only healing the past, but also lifting us upward to see the horizon ahead.

I often try to imagine a story that I tell myself about the legend of the great cathedral. The nobles and peasants who so many years ago pushed their separate carts filled with stones to build Chartres did so as individuals each with their own heavy load to bear. Each one made only an infinitesimally small contribution. But taken as a whole, that tiny contribution was sufficient to produce man's greatest work of living art, Chartres. But I like to imagine in the late afternoon with the light receding over the plain that they looked forward to the fellowship of others. They knew the great truth: we die as we dream, alone; but we only experience the small joys of this life in our love and communion with others.

Please forgive the ramblings of an old woman. They say wisdom comes with age, but what good is wisdom with so little life left to live with it? Your life and the lives of all of us on this continent have been uprooted by this war. It is a time for healing. Healing is a gift brought to us by others who love us unconditionally, even though at times we struggle in our isolation to be worthy of that love.

You and Camille are in my prayers,

Sister Esme

CHAPTER 28

▼

Ruck-a-tak, rick-a-tak, ruck-a-tak, rick-a-tak. The hypnotic sound of the night train from Paris to Lyon was a welcome diversion to the constant searing pain in Rennaut's left leg. "How ironic," he thought to himself staring at the discolored bandages around his calf. "I fought harder against the doctors who wanted to saw this damn thing off than against the Germans."

He had refused the morphine injections the other men had longed for on the wards because of his fearful memories of vacant stares on opium smokers' faces that he recalled seeing as a young man. He struggled to capture the precise words the old man in a Sudanese bazaar used to describe the opium smokers who stumbled into his coffee house each morning through the cheap strings of amber glass beads hanging in the doorway. "What was the translation of the phrase?" he wondered. "The 'seekers of death in life.' Yes. Well, that was no death at all."

He knew about death. The way to die was not in a slow-motion spiral that drained your dignity with each puff of an opium pipe. No, a bullet through the head was infinitely preferable.

Many of the men he saw on the long rows of the hospital wards suffered from the intense, paralyzing guilt over being a survivor, wondering over and over why they had been allowed to live and others not. In the first years of the war Allain had believed that his skill and knowledge as a soldier had been the difference in keeping him alive. As time went on, however, he knew this was a deceitful fantasy and that survival at the front was purely based on chance, like some great indifferent roulette wheel.

The war was now over for Allain, but equally significant was the fact that his life in the army was over as well. The army had formed his entire adult frame of reference and the measure of all things. There were no rules in war, but the army had rules and he would miss them. Its rules were flawed and arbitrary and at times cruel; nevertheless, there were written and unwritten codes of behavior. Allain had often existed in opposition to that defined way of life. In fact, he could even succeed by outwitting his superiors, bending the rules to suit his purposes in a grand game that he had played for over twenty years. And now he had his captain's bars to prove it.

The train seemed to relinquish all its strength as it groaned from exhaustion into the station. As he gazed out the window of his couchette, he was struck by the clash of the white clouds of steam and the black wrought iron arches with the station's enormous panes of glass turned into an ambiguous gray. He recalled for a moment how at the start of the war the troop train from Marseilles had stopped here to pick up the French officers for the Moroccan battalion. That too was a contrast that seemed jarring. Gone were the cheering crows of adoring girls with their sea of tricolors and bright white and red scarves. Gone were the mass of young Arab boys enraptured by the energy and complexity of the metropolis and caught up in the newness of a war with all its possibilities.

Those memories proved short-lived, and Allain began to notice a few loitering groups of soldiers returning from leave. They slouched at attention smoking in groups of twos and threes. He threw his green canvas duffel onto the quay and, nearly breathless from the pain in his leg, fought his way through the crowd onto the cobblestone pavement. A moment of dizziness and disorientation came over him and his entire perception of the scene at the station slowly changed its visual character. Against the nondescript black and white backdrop of the normal bustle of citizens in the great hall were stationary objects in vivid colors; men with legs and arms on their suits pinned up from missing limbs. The ghostlike figures turned one by one and began calling out to him, "Allain, Allain."

"Allain! Over here!" It was his mother Valerie. He was home in Lyon and the nightmare was over for now.

CHAPTER 29

▼

The Rennaut and Fleuret Bakery had been suppliers of fine bread to the most exclusive restaurants in Lyon for two generations. The sons and daughters of both families handled all aspects of the business: baking, distribution, and bookkeeping. The distinctive taste of its bread reflected not only a passion for the highest quality of its flour and yeast, but also on a method the families had perfected for baking the bread at exceptionally high heat. This shortened the baking time and gave the bread its distinctive firm, flaky crust and soft and richly flavorful center. The cost of the ingredients and fuel for the ovens, however, were higher than those of the other bakeries and only the leading restaurants were willing to pay the premium price. Lyon, unlike Paris, Rouen, and Marseilles, had fared poorly in obtaining government contracts for arms, uniforms, and munitions. Both patriarchs, Rennaut's father, Jean-Marie, and Charles Fleuret had died before the war. Within the three years after the start of the conflict, seven of the elite restaurants in Lyon had closed their doors and the ripple effect greatly reduced the profitability of the bakery. What made the financial crisis worse was their dwindling production due to a lack of manpower. Four of the five male family workers were now at the front, including Allain's cousin Jean-Claude and three of Fleuret's sons. The bakery required hard physical work over long hours, lifting the sixty-pound sacks of flour and stoking the fires at 3:00 AM to the right temperature. With half of the needed workers at the front and no available young men to replace them, the fortunes of the bakery seemed bleak.

In the carriage ride back to their home, Allain sensed the strain in his mother's voice from the financial pressures on the bakery. Valerie Rennaut had always been the emotional spark of the family, breaking the tedium of the bakery work with impromptu concerts with her accordion and fine singing voice. But as a widow at sixty-four with a failing business and a crippled son, she seemed withdrawn and distracted. A diminutive woman with large brown eyes and long gray hair knotted tightly behind her high forehead, Jean-Marie always called her his "singing angel." Allain remembered as a boy the languid Sunday dinners on the wooden table by the large fig tress with warm sensations of wine, cold tarragon chicken, and the humorous and often disparaging remarks from Charles and Jean-Marie about national politicians. It was difficult to see his mother in this new light knowing there was little he could do to help, apart from offering a small sum of money.

"My pension from the army as a captain is nearly 2000 francs a year. Surely that will help."

"It's good money after bad, my son. We're already losing 300 francs a month. We do not have enough workers to tend the ovens. All the boys are in the army and the Germans aren't quitting anytime soon. And just last week another restaurant, "The Swan"—you know, by the river, closed. And Allain you will have medical expenses to pay for that leg of yours. No, we must sell and sell quickly before there's nothing left."

That night at dinner they were joined by Fleuret's only daughter, Luce. At thirty-six, most neighbors in the quarter considered her well past the threshold of spinsterhood, and her total preoccupation with the bakery did little to dispel that notion. Her devotion to the bakery was profound and based on an extraordinary respect for Allain's father. At nineteen Luce became pregnant by a substitute schoolteacher. Despite his promises of marriage, he quickly disappeared as soon as she began to show. Her family disowned her, but not Jean-Marie Rennaut. He took care of all the arrangements and personally drove her by carriage to a remote farm in Brittany and arranged for her to stay with a childless farmer and his wife who would later adopt the child. He paid all of the expenses and procured the finest midwife in the area. Most importantly, he did not judge her. "You have done nothing wrong, my child. You will always have a home with my family and a job with the bakery. Your child will in due time become part of our family. Now you must be brave and do not cry, only know that the future will be brighter."

The baby was stillborn, yet for many months Luce did not know whether to feel grateful or sad. However, she knew in her heart that the goodness of Jean-Marie had redeemed her. When she returned to Lyon, she lived on her own from the money she earned at the bakery.

Luce was plain and cared little for fashion or men, but she was cheerful and animated with flashing gray-green eyes. She took care of the bakery's books, managed the inventories, and met regularly with the restaurant owners to ensure quality and prompt delivery. When the two patriarchs died, Luce essentially ran the business. With Valerie's deepening gloom, her quick wit and laughing smile tried to brighten things, but she knew firsthand the many financial challenges facing the bakery.

Allain was nearly a decade older and had not seen Luce for many years. He barely noticed her on the few times he went home on leave from the army, preferring to spend the limited time carousing with his friends. But he knew a leader when he saw one and immediately accepted her for her business acumen.

Allain spoke plainly at a kitchen table meeting with Luce and Valerie: "We should not decide to sell in haste until we have exhausted all possibilities. Things may look different in a month. What if your brothers, Marcel, Edouard, and Jean come home from the war with no jobs? How would that be? This bakery has been in business over forty years. We can carry on for a few months to sort this out. We will talk to the restaurant owners. They know and trust us. We will cut costs. In the meantime here is 500 francs. That should help us meet the payroll. Now, you'll excuse me; I must say goodnight."

Luce took Allain's hand and spoke next, "Bless you, Allain. You have been more than generous and I know that we will pay you back somehow. But first we must see to that leg of yours."

Valerie Rennaut was caught in a cycle of despair and anxiety about the bakery, the war, and her crippled son. She neglected to eat and stayed in her room for most of the day, refusing to go to the post office for fear of the mounting bills. Allain's leg grew worse, with pus draining from his calf and nightly fevers. At this point, Luce stepped in and took command of the bakery and Allain's health. She paid a neighbor to live in with Valerie to cook her favorite meals. She then moved Allain into a small cottage behind her house. Despite his grumbling and wariness of doctors, every week she would gingerly load Allain into the back of her carriage and take him to a different physician to try to find a treatment for his worsening infection in his leg. At first she went to the older, more experienced physicians in Lyon who were knowledgeable about treating war wounds. Their response was identical; amputation was the only effective treatment and delaying the inevitable risked sepsis and death from a bloodstream infection. She and Allain refused to accept this and Luce suggested a different tack, "Why don't we find a younger doctor, one who has a newer outlook and new ideas? These old retired surgeons are just stuck in the past."

Doctor Henri Werthe was struggling to make a go of it with his small surgical clinic on the fringe of Lyon's declining factory district. As a Jew, the upper classes were unimpressed by his exceptional surgical training at Montpellier and two years of apprenticeship in Paris. The workers and managers in the textile factory were his main clients. They were unsure and apprehensive about his newer methods of diagnosis and treatment. Unlike the elite society doctors on rue Faubourg, he had little interest in idle chatter with elderly ladies and placed marginal emphasis on bedside manner or outward appearances. Short and wiry, with his wavy auburn hair jutting out from the sides of his rounded glasses, Werthe was an anomaly among the Lyonnais medical establishment. Unlike the older physicians in the area, who routinely over prescribed for trivial aches and dubious pains, Werthe was not interested in indulging his patient's psychosomatic complaints, particularly if surgery was not indicated. Telling them that there was nothing wrong with them did not produce repeat visits and limited his practice.

As they walked onto the clinic waiting area, Allain and Luce were first struck by the row of empty wooden chairs. Seeing no one at first, they peered into a large adjoining room with a strange piece of equipment that was positioned above a table.

They were startled by a low-pitched voice behind them, "Quite remarkable, isn't it? It's one of only three Roentgen machines in all of Lyon. It takes pictures with the new X-rays you've no doubt heard about. We used this quite effectively in Paris. Pity there aren't more patients to benefit from this. Oh, I forgot to introduce myself, I'm Doctor Werthe, unless you are bill collectors, what seems to be the trouble?"

"It's his leg wound, Doctor. Allain was treated in the army hospitals before he was discharged, but it's infected and won't heal," replied Luce.

Werthe ushered him into an examining room and carefully unwrapped the bandages from Allain's leg. He seemed unperturbed by the malodorous stench of the necrotic tissue in the wound. After a lengthy examination, Werthe put down his stethoscope.

"And how often are the fevers? And the pain, what is the character of the pain?"

"The fevers were intermittent at first but seem to be nightly now. The pain is like a hot poker searing my leg and it's pretty constant."

"I will need to take an X-ray picture of your wound with the Roentgen machine. I want to see if there is still shrapnel in your wound. Without this I cannot properly advise you on a course of therapy."

After this was accomplished, Werthe washed his hands in the sink in the examining room and held the image up to the light of a small lamp. He then turned directly to Allain. "I'm sure that the doctors you consulted all told you the same thing. You have chronic osteomyelitis, which is a bone infection in the area of your wound. The conservative thing to do, of course, given your fevers, would be to simply amputate the leg. The more radical and more risky treatment is to, in fact, try to salvage your limb. There is still one large piece of shrapnel lodged partially in the leg bone, the tibia. In addition, much of your calf muscles have become inflamed and necrotic from the draining pus. If you are willing, there are three things we must do to. First, you must improve your nutrition. The fevers over time sap your appetite and this makes the healing of the wound far more difficult. You must force yourself to take strong beef broth and vegetables three times a day. Secondly, we must remove the dead muscle tissue before we operate. This will be done with leeches. Finally, when the wound is cleaned I must operate to remove the shrapnel guided by another X-ray picture. The chances of success are guarded, but there is a chance. If you agree with this plan of action I will begin immediately to place the leeches in the wound. I can assure you that this will be painless."

Allain intuitively had confidence in the doctor and readily agreed. Quite remarkably, just a week after the leeches were place in the wound all of the dead muscle was gone and the edges of the wound had changed from reddish black to a robust pink. Luce had made strong beef broth and vegetable soup and fed it to him three times a day. The morning of the operation Dr. Werthe took another X-ray, this time with a metal clamp taped to his leg in the approximate area of the shrapnel. He carefully measured on the X-ray the distance between the shrapnel and the clamp to guide the placement of his incision. After administering the ether anesthesia, he then scrubbed his hands with for several minutes and made an incision where the X-ray indicated the likely location of the shrapnel. Within just a few minutes of deliberate dissection he found the metallic foreign body, removed it with a clamp, and then irrigated the wound.

Dr. Werthe came out of the operating room and spoke with Luce as he pulled down his mask, "It went as planned and I was able to remove the large shrapnel fragment that I saw on the X-ray. So that is encouraging. But I caution you we will not know the true outcome for several weeks. It is likely that the operation has stirred up the infection and he may actually be a bit worse for a while. We will just have to see."

Allain's nightly fever and chills persisted for the next two weeks. Luce, however, maintained an outwardly cheerful pose as she cooked his broth, changed his bandages, and got him dressed for their afternoon carriage rides into the country. Allain was unlike other men she had met before and she sensed in him the admirable qualities of his father. He immediately accepted her as an equal in all regards. He repeatedly acknowledged how grateful he was to her for supporting him, his mother, and the bakery through this difficult time. Despite the incapacitating nature of his pain, Allain never complained. He told her he was determined to keep his leg not out of vanity, but out of a deep need to put the war behind him. The reason, he stressed, was that he was not willing to become a permanent victim of the war. It would be unbearable to be reminded of the horror of it all every time he tried to take a step. The war had been a great tragedy and he would never remotely understand the mentality of the men who sent other men to die in such a hideous fashion. He was driven by a great passion to get beyond a cycle of destruction and despair. Luce mixed Port with his evening vegetable stew to help him sleep and when that didn't work she read to him from newspapers until he drifted off. In the morning when she would come to light the fire in the cottage, make him coffee, and dress him, his response was always the same, he would take her hand and look her in the eye and say simply, "Thank you. You are very kind." She began to feel the presence of his father.

The beginning of the third postoperative week witnessed a gradual, but definite improvement in Allain's condition. The fevers and drenching sweats became intermittent and the previously constant pain occurred only when he tried to bear weight on his leg. A psychological transformation occurred in Allain that paralleled his physical improvement. When he regained his strength, was able to dress himself, and had obtained a measure of independence, Luce commented, "Well, I guess you won't be needing me any more. Isn't that wonderful?"

Allain tenderly replied, "No you are wrong, Luce. I need you more than ever and I am determined that the two of us will see these tough times through and that the bakery will survive. I can only do this with you." At night, alone in her room, Luce cried that she had finally met such a man.

The financial condition of the bakery, however, continued to deteriorate. The restaurant owners wanted to cut costs as well and were less willing to pay the higher price of the premium quality bread. The cost of coal had nearly doubled over the past year and no new workers applied for the five jobs listed in the Lyon papers. All of these problems were potentially surmountable, but the telegram from the front that told of the death of the Luce's oldest bother, Marcel, was a crippling blow.

Allain called a meeting with Valerie and Luce and began by telling a story from the war. "I was leading a patrol at dusk to capture the communications headquarters of the Bavarian battalion attacking us. Our blood was up because the Germans had just gassed and killed one of the finest soldiers I had ever served, Captain Robine. We wanted revenge and we were well armed and ready to die and anxious to take a few Germans with us. Something seemed wrong, however, with our position. Sayed, my corporal, quickly appraised the situation and told me that if we attacked at that moment we would be immediately surrounded and annihilated. As difficult as it was, we called off the attack, waited until dark, and retreated to our lines. Sayed had been right as we later found that the Germans had sent to the front a new battalion of reinforcements. The next day when the Brits jumped off and preoccupied them, we counterattacked the Boche and achieved our greatest victory in two years."

Valerie looked puzzled, "What are you trying to say, Allain?"

"I am saying that sometimes you have to retreat to ultimately win the battle. We must sell the business in Lyon, but hear me out now, baking is in our soul. We must move to Paris, where there are both first-class restaurants and plenty of men needing work."

Luce did not hesitate: "Our competitor Picard has just upped his offer. We can be packed and ready for Paris in a week. I hear the Right Bank is the place to be for fine bread."

Within two months both families moved to adjoining appartments in Paris, purchased new ovens, and contracted with five restaurants. Now all they needed was a half-dozen good men to do the work. Rennaut placed the following ad in *Paris Soir*:

> Captain Allain Rennaut, formerly of the 3d Moroccan Battalion, seeks out old comrades in arms demobilized from the war or any other hardworking men for honest work and honest pay for a newly opened bakery. All men report to 227 rue Laurent at 0900 on October 22.

That morning at 7:00 AM Luce was awakened by a rustling crowd milling beneath her window. She quickly put on her robe and rushed to the back room near the ovens where Allain was sleeping.

"Allain, Allain, please get up quickly. There are noises out there. I think it's a mob or the police."

Allain struggled and went downstairs to the front door. On the pavement and in the street were a dozen Arab men from the battalion.

Allain seemed overwhelmed to see so many of his old comrades, who surrounded him, hugging and cheering, "Sayed, Atah, Mustaf—my God, you've all come! Luce, please make a big pot of coffee."

Luce rushed to his side and whispered, "Allain, by my count there are twelve men out there. We need only three or four at the most. How will we find all these men standing out here jobs in our bakery?"

"I don't know how, Luce, but we will, Luce! Somehow we will!"

CHAPTER 30

▼

Zurich, December, 1917

Dear Carvalho,

I expect to return to Paris by train in the next few days and will contact you as soon as I arrive. I've accomplished some useful things here and am feeling better. My limp is nearly gone, and there is no longer any pain in my chest. I have purchased a few interesting paintings for Colonel Morrissey that I hope you'll enjoy for their playfulness. While I still haven't begun to paint yet, I think that there is a possibility that I may try in the near future; I will want to see Rennaut, so please tell him of my arrival. I received the news of the death of Camille's husband. One of the countless tragedies of this war. Sister Esme wrote to me, as I'm sure you know. Perhaps I will visit Camille as well.

Looking forward to seeing you,
Michel

CHAPTER 31

▼

Luce and Allain found that breaking into the baking business in Paris was far more challenging than expected. In addition, the dozen Arab men from the regiment now on the books strained the payroll considerably. It was true there were many more high-end restaurants in Paris, but they all seemed unwilling to change there suppliers after having built up relationships with bakeries over generations. The innumerable sidewalk bistros were far less interested in the higher cost of the bread from the Boulangerie Lumiere. To keep all the men busy, Allain rented the adjoining vacant storefront and although he had never baked a pastry in his life opened a patisserie. They hired several pastry chefs in the course of a month, only to have them leave for lucrative hotel jobs. Undaunted, Allain forged ahead and from books tried to make an assortment of pies, cookies, and tarts. They all failed miserably and even the children on the crowded street turned down the free samples.

Everything seemed a failure at this junction. Except for the éclairs. Allain by accident somehow got the recipe wrong and added many more egg whites and vanilla than called for. He recognized his mistake and was about to throw out the entire batch when Luce suddenly came through to the kitchen with several bills in her hand and remarked, "Whatever is that divine smell?"

"Oh, it's just my latest triumph of an éclair," said Allain jokingly.

Luce put down her papers, pulled an éclair off the cooling rack, and took a bite. "My goodness Allain. I've underestimated your skills all this time. This is without doubt the most delicious éclair ever produced by human hands. You must immediately write down what you did to make such a light and heavenly thing!"

And so the business began to turn around. The patisserie specialized only in éclairs, all kinds of éclairs. Allain had the idea of using the idle Arab men as street vendors to sell the éclairs from pushcarts around all the famous tourist attractions in the neighboring arrondissements. Carts were loaded up by 7:00 AM for distribution and they were all back by noon to take on a second batch. Each time they sold an éclair the men gave away a small business card advertising the bakery. It started to work, but what pushed them over the top was converting the patisserie into a small café that sold coffee and tea with the éclairs. Soon all the fashionable women out to do their shopping would have an éclair with a pot of tea and then go next door to buy their bread from the bakery. Within three months, Allain and Luce were able to pay all the men each week and put aside a small profit.

After one particularly hectic Saturday afternoon, Luce sat down for a rest when she detected something strange in the back of the café. She noticed that two of the men were dressed in their finest starched white waiter costumes, and she then overheard Allain calling her to a table in the back. She got up and saw Allain offering her a chair at a small table set with a fine lace tablecloth and a bottle of champagne. Allain was dressed in his officer's finest and was flanked by the rest of the men in their impeccably pressed uniforms. A single red rose was placed next to an elegant plate of china that held a single éclair covered in gold leaf.

"What's this all about, Allain?" she said taking her seat.

"This occasion, among other things, my dear, is to celebrate the sale of our one thousandth éclair. And I have chosen a very, very special éclair for you to try. But this is such a special éclair of which you must take very tiny bites using first your knife and fork. That, of course, is to enable you to appreciate the exceptional flavor. Shall we then?"

Luce wiped off the flour from her hands on her apron and picked up her knife and fork. As she began to cut into the éclair she was distressed to suddenly hit a hard object. She carefully cleared away the custard from the hard object with her fingers and lifted up a gold band with a single diamond. As Allain offered a tentative, "Then will you, Luce?"

She gasped and held her breath. Then she nodded yes through her tears to the exaggerated applause from the men.

CHAPTER 32

▼

Carvalho was there to meet him as the night train pulled into Paris. "You are much in demand, my boy," he said as he embraced Michel. "First, there is the matter of Rennaut's wedding, and you just received a letter from Father Dierot about some sort of an invitation in Valcourt, but the most urgent thing you must attend to is Sister Esme. She has recently taken ill with influenza. I just received a telegram from Camille this morning. I spoke with Dr Morrissey on the telephone, and he informed me that the entire hospital is full with American soldiers ill and dying from Spanish influenza. He has been working day and night to identify the microbe that is responsible for the epidemic, but unfortunately the doctors are powerless to do anything. The infection seems to kill the very young and the very elderly. That is what most concerns Camille. I am sorry to bombard you with all of this at this time, Michel. Now you will come back to my apartment to spend the night and rest. I've made the travel arrangements for you to go to Courville tomorrow."

Michel was so tired when he woke that he had little time to collect his thoughts on the morning train to Chartres, but as the train approached the plains of Beauce, he sprung to the window and was delighted at the sight of the cathedral's spires rising in the distance. It still stirred in him the old feelings. The once-familiar surroundings of the town, however, were different somehow and it seemed a small village compared to Zurich. He had to wait for over an hour for a single taxi at the station. Gone were the horse-drawn carriages ferrying people to the orphanage and the outlying hamlets. The now dusty field behind the station Michel recalled had been the site of daily farmer's market that by this time on a May morning would be frenetic with activity. He walked to the other side of the station to see a new butcher's shop and several small stores selling religious items. "Was it here, I wonder?" Michel said to himself trying to recall the exact spot near the stall where he sold his painted postcards on Sunday afternoons.

Some things, however, had not changed. The unpaved road leading to the orphanage had not improved and there were deep gashes in the mud from tire marks following the spring rains. The ride was jarring and he was apprehensive about what he would find.

Although he had telephoned Sister Monique to tell her of his plan to visit, there was no one at the gate to greet him upon his arrival. There was much less activity than he remembered, with only a few children and nuns walking by the dormitory courtyard, who took no notice of him. He was surprised to find that the old infirmary by the office building was closed and the door locked. Michel walked into the office and asked a woman he did not recognize if he could speak with Sister Monique.

"I am afraid Mr. Hassan that Sister Monique is occupied at the moment with the epidemic. My name is Sister Francesca. May I help you?"

"I hope so. I was here many years ago as a child. I understand that Sister Esme is ill and I came to visit her," said Michel.

"Oh, you are a friend of Sister Esme's. Of course, let me take you to her. I'm quite sure Sister Monique is there as well."

As they walked into the courtyard, Michel inquired, "Why isn't Sister Esme in hospital? I understand she is desperately ill with the flu."

"The district hospital in Chartres is completely full, I'm afraid. We alone have some twenty of our sickest children in hospital there, to say nothing of the towns-people. It's the same in Paris and all over I'm told. It's as bad as the war they tell me. Maybe worse in some ways. It's the children I'm thinking of. Many of our children have died in the hospital and here at the orphanage. It's been terribly hard on all of us. Of course, Sister Esme, who was caring for the sickest children before she became ill, has refused to leave. There were so many stricken with the flu that our small infirmary was overwhelmed. We've converted the first two floors of the classroom building into our own makeshift hospital. The doctor comes every day from Chartres, but we are very short of nurses. It just seems that there is nothing to be done to save them. Some of the smaller children expire in just a few days.

"Here we are. I'm not allowed in, as I interact with people outside the orphan-age—the suppliers and workers—and the doctor wants to minimize the chance of further transmission. You'll have to wash your hands in the basin inside the front door and wait for the nurse to let you through."

"Thank you, Sister Francesca. You've been most kind," said Michel.

As he entered the ground floor and began to wash his hands in the basin of dilute carbolic acid, Michel saw the doctor down the hallway putting away his stethoscope into his bag. Michel came up to him and asked, "Excuse me doctor, I am a friend of Sister Esme. How is her condition?"

"A serious case, I'm afraid. You'll notice the bluish tinge. That's the telltale cyanosis from the pneumonia. Usually a sign of death in forty-eight hours. And at her age. Well, you'd better see her now. She's a bit short of breath, but alert for the time being. Can't promise you more than that. Nothing I can do really. No pain or need of morphine just yet. She's in the small room just there off the main ward. But you'll have to excuse me. Rounds to make in the hospital, for all the good it'll do."

Michel entered the makeshift ward and saw two long rows of children being attended to by nuns and nurses, who took no notice of him. He entered the side door off the ward and saw Camille and Sister Monique sitting in chairs by the bedside next to the window. Camille rose, kissed him on the cheek, and then held Michel's hand tightly.

Sister Monique held Sister Esme's hand and spoke first, "Michel, I hardly recognized you." Then turning to the bed she spoke into Sister Esme's ear, "It's Michel, he's come back from the war. He's come back to see us."

Sister Esme raised herself up a bit in bed and said haltingly in a gasping voice, "So you're here, are you? Good. Not much time. We have to talk. Now, Sister, please go and get me that tea, will you?"

Sister Monique replied, "Why, of course." And slowly got up and left.

Sister Esme began, "Good. Just the three of us. Sister Monique's mad at me. Oh, not just that I'm dying, but that I am holding on to this and not the Bible."

Michel saw next to Sister's Esme's right hand a leather-bound ancient text. He thought he recognized it.

"It's the one you showed me of the saints many years ago," said Michel.

"And what about the saints? Do you remember?"

"They were different. They seemed to have the expressions of real people," answered Michel.

"Yes, and that's why I treasure it above all others. All the other illustrated texts strive for beauty. An idealized beauty. It's not real. The saints...well, in those books they look like the angels and cherubs you see floating above them. They're no different. But in this book there is a vision of something else. What do you suppose that is, Michel?"

"I don't know, that the saints are of this world perhaps."

"Yes. Yes, that's it. I don't know if there is a God—with all this suffering, all this needless suffering. But I do know there are holy people. I have known them and so have you. Some are recognized by the church and called saints. Other saints like Tommasso are just people. The point is to bend toward the light, in this world, the only world we know. Now please, dear, a little water."

After struggling to take a sip of water, Sister Esme continued, "As a painter and a singer, you both know what distinguishes man from all the other animals. One thing, as we have seen in this war, is man's alarming capacity for cruelty. But fortunately there remain two positive needs. I would say the first is his need for art—to extend man's feeble vision in trying to make sense of things. But I will tell you the other even greater need is the need to love. Just think about that for a moment, you two. Now let an old woman have minute of peace. You both have much to talk about."

Michel and Camille left the room and started slowly walking beyond the courtyard. Michel asked, "What are your plans now, and is it true that you are abandoning your opera career?"

Camille replied as they strolled that she no longer felt the need to travel and that with the death of Robert and his brother she wished to return to the only family she had known here at Courville. She was close enough to Paris to go to the occasional opening, but the stage was a life of superficial living for the moment. She would stay in Courville, give voice lessons, and teach the orphanage choir.

Camille noticed a slight residual limp in Michel's gait and asked him how his wounds were.

"Improving each month, although I don't quite have the stamina to do long walks or go cycling as I used to," he responded.

The word "cycling" hung in the air and in silence was a reminder of their happy past.

Michel continued, "Yes, my physical wounds are better, but I am still not well. There is much we have to say to each other, but I know now is a time for your grieving and a time for me to begin healing. The difficulty is that I really don't know where to begin."

"Begin by being with the people you care about the most," offered Camille.

"Yes, I suppose you're right."

They walked in silence back to the makeshift infirmary and saw Sister Monique coming out of Sister Esme's room and closing the door. She held the ancient leather text in her left hand by her side and when she saw Michel and Camille simply bowed her head and gave the sign of the cross.

CHAPTER 33

▼

The planning of the wedding of Allain and Luce was well underway by the time Michel arrived back in Paris. The café and bakery were now generating a modest profit, but the practical and ever frugal Luce refused to rent a separate hall for the reception arguing, "We'll paint and fix up the café and use that for the reception. Think of how much better it will be for the customers."

That weekend they closed the café, and Allain, Sayed, and Atah patched up all the cracks in the walls. When Allain asked Luce what color she wanted for the décor, she replied, "White seems appropriate for the bride, don't you think? I'll soften the effect with some nice powder blue curtains."

But by the time they had paid in advance for some new table and chairs, the champagne, the caterer, and the musicians, there was only a little money left over for the honeymoon to Normandy. The curtains would have to wait and the large white walls seemed stark even after the new furniture was arranged in the room. Luce was angry at herself at picking white as the color. "It's so cold in a way, don't you think so, Allain?"

"Nonsense, after three glasses of champagne and a couple of lively dances the whole place will be aglow with the warmth of the happy occasion. Even your Aunt Matilde will warm up to it!" Allain shot back.

But the austere white walls continued to prey on Luce's imagination. The apprehension was only broken late that afternoon when Michel arrived. Sayed, who was at the door, didn't recognize him at first without his officer's uniform, but once he heard his voice the disbelief gave way to joy. Allain and the men were overcome to see him, and even Luce was struck by the reception he received. Allain soon broke into the champagne for the wedding and Michel offered this toast, "I can't tell you how happy I am for the both of you. I promise you I will be back here next Saturday for the wedding. I'll save my more formal toast until then. I have a small trip to go on for a few days, but I'll be back in Paris in time to get you a suitable present. To your happiness!"

CHAPTER 34

▼

The handwritten note from Father Dierot was left on the nightstand in his old room at Carvalho's. Weary from the long wedding celebration, Michel sat on the edge of the bed and tried to decipher the message:

> Much news to tell you about the abbey, but you must come and see for your-self. Your presence is requested in Valcourt at noon on Monday. Please come to my old cottage and I will explain it all to you. Intensely looking forward to seeing you there.
>
> —Father Jacques Dierot

Tired as he was, Michel left for the Gare du Nord train station early the next morning puzzled at the meaning of the note, but strangely compelled to see what it was all about. He had scarcely thought of Valcourt, Father Dierot, and the abbey at Montebrillion in the many months recovering in hospital and then in Zurich. He thought to himself looking out the window of the train that in this short time of two years not much would have changed in this small village. There were countless such villages in northern France and Belgium devastated by the war that would take decades to recover. Their once rich farmland had been reduced to a wasteland from years of shelling and was scarred by miles of trenches and fortifications. Underground dugouts used by millions of soldiers on the Western Front were now home to rats and feral dogs. Michel knew that this land, however barren at present, might recover in time—the impersonal renewal of nature. But what of the renewal of the human spirit he wondered? Even now, two years after the fighting, pockets of saplings and brush were starting to reappear, but the thousands of sons killed would not come back to till the land. The few surviving boys who would come back from the war would not be the same. Such farm villages like Valcourt, tucked far away from the central governments that allocated the reconstruction money, would be far down the list of the countless projects needing restoration. And the small abbey would require considerable resources from a church likely to be distracted by the large cathedrals badly in need of repair. No, he thought to himself, the best one could hope for was a small sign of a rekindling of the spirit that would point the way for the decades' long effort to rebuild. The irony was that some villages, like Valcourt, that had been of immense strategic importance during war, were now all but forgotten once the guns were silenced. No, Michel thought, if any meager renewal was to happen it would have to be done by the inhabitants of such villages and be done on their own.

But Michel had not counted on an unlikely factor: the persuasive powers of a stubborn old woman who would not accept the futility of reconstruction. That woman was, in fact, the widow Mrs. Ornier, Father Dierot's childhood sweetheart. Madame Ainais Ornier at sixty-seven had much the same energy and cantankerousness she did at twenty-seven when out of despair she married a doddering, wealthy estate owner in marginal health. Dierot had not proposed after ten years of courtship and his vague discussions about joining the priesthood pushed her completely over the edge. Soon widowed after marriage, she preferred to have little to do with men. When her mother died, she sold her large manor house and moved to town. She had lost two grandsons in the war and her only daughter to the influenza outbreak. Her grief seemed boundless when a prelate from the archbishop came to the village and announced that there would be no parish priest for the foreseeable future to comfort the villagers. But her grief turned to anger when, at a town meeting of all the adult villagers at the mayor's house, the church emissary, Father Bezin, announced that the decision was made not to restore the abbey but to clear the remains and sell off what they could of the debris.

Ainais Ornier slowly got up from her seat in the back of the living room and after decisively clearing her throat said in a clear forceful voice, "What do you mean you will tear down the abbey and sell it for scrap? Do you think our stained glass windows are just debris?"

"Madame, the abbey is a ruin," Father Bezin replied. "However, some of the rubble may still be valuable to sell off. It is not possible for the church to rebuild the abbey. The cost is prohibitive. And where would we find the workmen after the war? Surely you understand, Madame?"

"No, I do not understand, Father. I refuse to understand. The stained glass windows are still there untouched as beautiful as ever. We should restore the abbey. We will restore the abbey," replied Mrs. Ornier to the affirmative murmurs of the assembled crowd.

Father Bezin tried to restrain his frustration at this point and continued in a condescending tone, "But, Madame, even by some miracle if you were able to rebuild the abbey, it would be pointless. The bishop has reassigned the parish priest for this village. There would be no one to say mass. It would be an empty building without a priest."

Mrs. Ornier fired back, "Then we shall recall Father Dierot out of retirement until the church sees the error of its ways. He shall not refuse my offer." A gentle murmur rippled among the villagers.

Father Bezin now was losing his patience, "Fine then, Madame, recall Father Dierot if you like. He can say mass over the rubble if you like, but you will not receive one sou from the church."

"Then we shall have to do it ourselves. I will donate the first 1000 francs. Thank you, Father Bezin, but we have work to do," Mrs. Ornier replied to the excited assembly.

As the disgruntled emissary walked down the center aisle to exit the room, Mrs. Ornier rose to speak, "I shall telegram Jacques tomorrow. He will be delighted to be of service again. All who agree to join in this effort meet me at 8:00 at the south wall of the abbey. We will first remove any useful lumber from the trenches for anyone to use. Then we will fill in the trenches to remove that blight from our fields. Then we shall start rebuilding the abbey. I cannot promise you will be paid for your effort. But you will find much reward in this work."

The word went out all over the Ancre River valley about the restoration of the abbey. The first morning eight men showed up with tools and wheelbarrows to reclaim the trenches. Fortunately, the weather was remarkably fine. The next day there were fourteen and the next day twenty-seven. By the end of the week, fifty men and boys were busily at work pulling out the lumber and filling in the trenches and dugouts. The village women set up tents in the old officer's mess by the road and made a field kitchen. Mrs. Ornier ruled the scene with complete authority and each day laid out a plan of action for what needed to be accomplished. She bought the first ten wheelbarrows herself, and then other donated equipment suddenly started to appear. By the end of month, over a hundred seventy men from as far away as fifty miles were busily restoring the landscape. Sometimes they worked for a day or two, sometimes for a week. Many left their farms completely and lived in tents by the abbey.

The trenches around the abbey were completely filled in six weeks. The garden society planted saplings of willow and birch by the river trenches and created a flower-lined pathway where the artillery had been set up. Then they started to clear the stones from abbey and pile them in an orderly fashion. Mrs. Ornier made an edict: "We will use as much of the original stone as possible. I want an inventory of each stone where it lies so we can restore it. We will first rebuild the foundation of the walls around the stained glass windows to stabilize this."

Of course, Father Dierot was delighted to return and escape from his sister's chaotic household in Amiens. Retirement for him had been a time of depression. The feeling of being useful again was like a tonic to him. The fact that Ainais had personally contacted him was even sweeter. At his age he was not able to do the physical work, but he provided an even greater service to the effort. He used his writing skills to pen endless articles in the local newspapers and spread the word of the restoration effort all over northern France. Soon the word got out and there were numerous small donations pouring into Mrs. Ornier's charity fund. Equally important, there were now over two hundred fifty workers on the project living with farmers throughout the valley. Men came from Flanders and Belgium and all over France. Arab men of the 3d Moroccan worked side by side with doctors, accountants, farmers, and their wives in an intense communal effort.

The restoration reached a critical stage, however, when the walls had been finished. There was no one who knew precisely how to put up a vaulted roof over this abbey. There were photographs and sketches of the interior of the original ceiling that were an excellent guide. Architects from Paris and Normandy were consulted, but there was no one who knew quite how to recreate the original roof.

Dierot summed up the situation thus: "I suppose that the skill of erecting vaulted ceilings died with the men of the Middle Ages. We are at a difficult juncture, Mrs. Ornier. If the roof is not put up soon the winter rains could undermine our entire effort."

She replied with equanimity "Well, it is up to you, Jacques, to use your pen to find the man who can do it. Use your creativity."

Father Dierot decided to place notices in a variety of European journals of architecture and classical archeology searching for an architect with the right talents. But as July ended and August began and the months of good weather were almost over, the entire enterprise seemed at risk. The freshly poured foundations might wash away in a November deluge.

The man to do the job was not French and arrived with little fanfare in a black Mercedes sedan. There was much confusion at first about the man because of his thick German accent. The individual who emerged from the car was the retired German Captain and university Professor Franz Schulnitz. He was very same artillery officer who had at the battle of Valcourt refused General von Vietz's order to fire on his own Royal Guards. Franz had risked court-martial to save his men and he had no compunction to risk German public opinion in the restoration of the abbey.

Despite the August humidity the small man with a mustache and thinning gray hair dusted off his three-piece wool suit as he nodded to his chauffeur. With typical German directness he inquired, "Who, may I ask, is in charge?"

When presented to Mrs. Ornier he tilted his head gallantly and spoke. "Allow me to introduce myself, Madame. I am Professor Franz Schulnitz, Professor Emeritus of Medieval Architecture at the University of Freiburg. I read your notice in the architectural journal and I decided to make the trip and investigate the situation. Church ceilings of the early medieval period are my academic specialty and I might add, something of a passion. I did my thesis on the ceiling at the Cluny Chapel, which I believe is a reasonable facsimile of your abbey. I am quite familiar with your remarkable abbey as it turns out, having looked at it through my field glasses from the German lines every day for five months. If I can be of technical assistance in the building of the roof, I would be more than delighted to be of use."

"Professor," Mrs. Ornier replied, "the pleasure is entirely ours. We will rely on you, Professor, not only for your technical assistance, as you put it, but to be in charge of the entire roof construction. Now you and your man will stay with me as my guest in my house in the village."

"That is most kind of you, Madame Ornier. I am a bit tired at the moment, but would like very much this evening to review any and all historical documents, drawings, or sketches you have pertaining to the original abbey. In the morning I would like to see all of the construction foremen here at 7:00 for a meeting. We will undoubtedly be on a tight schedule. I want to let you know that we will need a great deal of the original stones, cement, and lumber for scaffolding."

Mrs. Ornier replied, "I find your directness refreshing, Professor. We will not disappoint you. Now please have your chauffeur follow me in my car."

Fortune favored the brave, and the heavy rains came late that fall just as the last tiles were being positioned on the beautifully constructed roof. Professor Schulnitz, however, proved to be a formidable rival to Father Dierot for Mrs. Ornier's affections. However, the appearance in early November of a certain Mrs. Franz Schulnitz, attempting to reclaim her husband for the Christmas holidays, quickly restored equilibrium to the situation.

The basic exterior construction of the abbey had been finished, but extensive work remained in completing the interior, with its elaborate marble floor and intricately carved altars. Father Dierot estimated that at the present rate of donations and the pace of work required to finish the job, the abbey would take a full year to finish. He called together a meeting of Mrs. Ornier and all the workmen inside the abbey to discuss a fitting ceremony in a year's time to commemorate the restoration.

"Future generations need to know what was done here." Dierot began. "We need to plan for a formal ceremony to mark the grand occasion of the opening of the abbey. In addition to all those high church officials who said it couldn't be done, we need to invite the usual political dignitaries. But we need to think of something in addition—a special plaque or commissioned piece of art. Anyone have any ideas?"

A man from the Troisième rose to speak, "Hassan, Major Hassan, was always making beautiful sketches of the ruined abbey and its windows. Four or five of them at least. Why not have him do a painting?"

"A commissioned painting of the abbey from Major Hassan. What an excellent idea!"

As the early morning train fled the row houses of the grimy Paris suburbs and headed into the northern countryside, Michel saw isolated pockets of old men and boys in their wagons inspecting the fences along the gray-brown fields of winter. By eight o'clock it was a cold but unusually bright, sunlit morning and in a short time the train approached the trench lines along the old northern front. The names on the signposts of the villages and towns were now familiar to Michel as wartime depots, staging areas, or battlefronts. There was nothing distinctive about these quiet forgotten hamlets now. Michel saw an abandoned tractor flung on its side with its rusting wheel rims sticking out from a ditch like some fallen warrior too laden with armor to get up on his steed.

On the outskirts of Valcourt, Michel began to sense a different scene. He noticed that there were numerous tents along the tracks with gray smoking fires. They seemed at first to him to be haphazardly stationed rear guard troops, but then he noticed women cooking breakfast, tending the fires. He could not understand why people in the winter would be living this way. As the train approached the station, Michel saw a young boy in a red shirt racing and waving at the train. Although Michel only caught glimpses of him as he came in and out of view running up the sides of the embankment, he appeared to be flying a kite and his burst of energy seemed to defy the winter's chill.

Father Dierot was at the station to meet him. "It is a welcome sight to see you, Major. I know you have been out of the country and in Switzerland for some time now and you may not be aware what is happening here. Let me offer you some coffee in my makeshift office at the end of the street and I will explain."

As they walked Dierot explained, "Thanks to a prominent resident in the town, a Mrs. Ornier, a massive restoration has been underway to rebuild the abbey. The medieval stained glass windows survived the war intact and so rather than just scrap the whole abbey, literally hundreds of men and women through France, Belgium, and yes, even Germany, heeded the call and have helped with the project. New foundations were poured this fall and the walls and roof have been completed in record time. In short, the exterior of the abbey is nearly finished and now there are craftsmen from all over Europe working on the interior. We estimate that it will take about a year to finish the job. Now this is where you come in."

"This is remarkable news, Father. I'm excited to see the abbey restored, of course. But what do you want me to do?"

"Ah, even at this early date we are planning a huge celebration to dedicate the reopening of the abbey. The point is, Major, we want you to do a grand painting of the abbey as you remember it in ruins during the war. You see, we want future generations to take strength from the miracle that the windows endured and to acknowledge the incredible effort made by the countless ordinary men and women who sacrificed to rebuild it."

"It seems a very worthwhile endeavor, Father, and it is, of course, a great honor for you to even consider me, but their are many professional painters far more talented."

"Ah, there you are mistaken, Major. You are the ideal person to do this painting. You will paint this from the heart. We know of your love for the abbey and its windows. You lived through the experience of the war and the miraculous preservation of the windows. You are unquestionably our choice for the commission. Now before you make any hasty decision let us just take a stroll over to the abbey. I think you'll see some people you'll remember."

It was little more than a fifteen-minute walk to the abbey. They walked along the path of the newly filled-in trenches and as they reached the crest of a small knoll in front of the abbey Michel could see that a large crowd had gathered. The crowd approached the two men in silence and then parted as Dierot and Michel grew nearer. Soon there were shouts of "Major! Welcome back, Major!" Michel saw arms raise in the crowd in what appeared to be a salute. Michel stopped and the crowd gathered around him.

Michel saw a face he thought he recognized. "Major, it's Lieutenant Atah. There is Mustaf and over there is…"

The crowd closed around Michel until Father Dierot intervened and in a loud voice said, "There will be plenty of time for reunions, but now we must give the Major a chance to see the abbey." The crowd then parted as the two men made their way to the abbey. Once inside, the fading winter sun did not do justice to the windows, but they were still beautiful to Michel.

At the train station that evening Michel simply said to Dierot, "I was very moved by what I saw today. I will think about things, Father. There is much to consider and lately I have been distracted from my painting, but I will let you know."

Michel spent the night at Carvalho's and in the morning Carvalho brought him a tray of coffee and fresh croissants. "You know, when I was a boy and a young man, my Russian nanny would come into my room like this with my breakfast and look at me and say, 'My dreams were good. It will be a good day today, Master.' And for some reason, looking at you I feel like saying the same thing. Tell me about your trip to the abbey."

"They want to commission me to do a large oil painting of the abbey as it was in the war, but I will tell you about that later. First, do you know if Rennaut has left for the holidays?" asked Michel.

"Yes, both he and Luce left for Lyon this morning and they won't be back for a week. He did invite you to Lyon to have Christmas, as you'll recall. You've been neglecting him a bit I fear after the wedding."

"Yes, well, it's better that he's away. I will need your help and a lot of supplies—paints, brushes, and drop cloths. Do you think you can manage that and lend me the delivery truck from the gallery? I want to take everything to the café. Is that blank wall in the front still painted all white?"

"Yes," said Carvalho, "that wall at the café is still that stark white that troubles Luce. However, I fear not for long. The keys to the delivery truck are on the hall table. The men in the bakery will let you into the café."

"Oh and Carvalho, I need a blank postcard and some watercolors before I leave."

For the next three days Michel lived at the café and had his meals brought in by the workmen cleaning the bakery ovens. He spent the entire time planning and then painting a mural that took up the entire front wall of the café. It was laborious at first reliving the memories, but then the images flowed out in a joyous torrent. The mural was of the ruined abbey and its stained glass windows. It was painted entirely from memory. At the base of the crumbling walls were all of the men he had cared so deeply about in the battalion. Rennaut was there with Mansour and Captain Robine, as well as Atah, Sayed, Mahmoud, and many others. The abbey and its windows were cast in light and shadow but the men's faces shone in the sunlight. The last thing he painted was a small postcard done is watercolors.

Carvalho was standing in the doorway as Michel was cleaning up. "Quite impressive, I'd say. Pity the masterpiece can't be transported to Valcourt and save you the trouble of doing it all over again. Now I'll take you home."

"Yes, but I must first make a telephone call."

The phone call was placed to the orphanage in Courville. Michel stood in the hallway of bakery and spoke into the large mouthpiece on the wall. "Yes, Madame, it is quite important. I need you to interrupt her during choir practice."

He waited anxiously until she came on the line. "Camille, is that you?"

"Michel, are you all right?"

"Yes, finally, for the first time in many years. When can I see you?"

"Right away. Tomorrow?" replied Camille.

"Tomorrow, then; I have a gift for you."

The painted postcard he left on hall table of Carvalho's apartment was a landscape surrounding the great cathedral at Chartres. In the sunlight in the foreground lying among the flowing fields of wheat were two small figures.

978-0-595-37696-4
0-595-37696-7

Printed in the United States
94551LV00003B/165/A

9 780595 376964